ALLIANCE
Volume Three

Annihilation

Avenger

JAMBREA JO JONES

Alliance Volume Three
ISBN # 978-1-78184-552-8
©Copyright Jambrea Jo Jones 2012
Cover Art by Posh Gosh ©Copyright 2012
Interior text design by Claire Siemaszkiewicz
Total-E-Bound Publishing

.

Total-E-Bound Publishing books by Jambrea Jo Jones:

Alliance Volume One
Retribution
Salvation

Alliance Volume Two
Freedom
Reward

Alliance Volume Three
Annihilation
Avenger

Seeds of Dawn Volume One
Dreams
Secrets

Seeds of Dawn Volume Two
Inequities
Origins

Seeds of DawnVolume Three
Redemption
Absolution

Semper Fi
Magnus
Ben

Dark Encounters
Dominate Me
Feel Me

Love by Design
Wishing Star
Stealing Michael
Tell Me Now
A Fistful of Emmett
Rayne's Wild Ride

ANNIHILATION

Dedication

To Nancy — Gill thanks you.
To all those who love sci-fi and a bit of man lovin'.
And to Joy.

Chapter One

'I WANT YOU.'

The old vintage recruitment sign with the image of Uncle Sam on it mocked Ricardo Clark. The finger pointed in his direction. Someone had marked out the part that said 'for the U.S. Army' and written over it with 'for the Alliance', some new form of government that had taken over power when the old government had crumbled.

Not that he had to worry. He'd been discharged years ago because of some stupid asthma thing and now he was a hundred pounds overweight, give or take a few pounds. Who would really 'want' him? He should have been able to stay in, but the military was overcrowded. They'd stopped recruiting after they pulled out of the Middle East and were looking at reasons to let go soldiers. Hell, with all the advancements in medicine he could have had his asthma cleared up in no time, but he didn't fight it. Not like he should have done. He had a place to go, others didn't, and they needed the stability of working for the government.

Rico continued his walk to the bakery. The only thing he was good for was eating a few doughnuts before going to his boring data entry job. After the big flood in 2050 there were tons of data that needed re-entering and a lot more of it lost. With his military career he had the necessary clearances to process the sensitive data so he was pretty secure in his job, unlike some others. It sucked, but it paid the bills. The homeless population was bigger than ever. It also kept his mom off his back. She was always asking him when he was going to find a nice boy and settle down. She'd bring up the old 'I helped fight for your right to marry whoever you want, now do something about it and make me proud. I want grandkids!' Rico didn't even know if he liked kids, not that it was an option now anyway. He was single and barely making ends meet. The job might have been steady, but it wasn't high-paying.

Before he was born there had been a big fight over government involvement in same-sex marriage and his parents had been in the 'trenches' as it were, fighting to make changes. Finally the government had passed a bill stating that it would take no part in deciding who a person could or could not marry and that each state had to abide by this bill, allowing people to marry whoever they wanted to. Or something like that. Rico couldn't remember the exact wording, but the gist of it was that same-sex couples could get married and have that marriage recognised wherever they went.

There had been a big outcry and some churches had taken a big stand, but, all in all, after a few years, no one really cared and it was business as usual. Still, there were the hatemongers out there, but as time passed they faded away from the spotlight. When

Rico had hit puberty it was all old news and there were different things to fight over. The churches prayed over the state of the world and blamed the rest of the nation for the coming apocalypse. Turned out it was a flood, not zombies taking over. The church still took credit saying their God was bringing down the sinners of the world. They never could come up with an explanation for how their congregations weren't spared.

Rico didn't really care because faith didn't really fit into what he wanted out of his life. He had big plans, like with his military career. It was supposed to be his ticket to law enforcement. He was thinking CIA or FBI. Now he was a glamorous clerk sitting behind a desk and clacking away at a keyboard all day.

He finally reached the shop and walked in.

"Rico! Your usual?" The owner winked at him.

Rico nodded and bellied up to the counter to wait for his order. It should've made him sad that the pastry people knew him, but he was hungry and running late. He didn't have time to be upset about a predicament of his own making. No one let him get so out of shape. That was all on him.

There was a new guy behind the counter and Rico couldn't stop staring. He was rugged and lean with short blond hair that stood on end and bright green eyes. He had scruff on his face and a shiner, like he'd gone a couple of rounds in a fight. But that wasn't what caught Rico's gaze. It was the black plugs in his ears and the tattoos running up and down each arm. They were colourful and he wanted a closer look, even leaned over the counter a bit before he caught himself. He could make out some sort of creature's head on his right shoulder in a dark red with black horns and it looked like wisps of smoke tied everything together.

There were a few other things, but he couldn't make them out without getting closer. On the other arm were a koi fish and cherry blossoms and other small tattoos.

But a man like that wouldn't look twice at the fat blob he'd become. Maybe when he was still in the military Rico'd have had the balls to approach him. Now he just took his sweets and left the bakery.

The city looked better than it had in years and he enjoyed his walk, taking a big bite of the gooey confection. The weather was nice, the sun shining. He was actually sweating a bit, the hazard of his extra pounds. For the first time he thought maybe he should do something about it. He thought back to the blond with those tattoos and threw his doughnuts into the next trash bin he found, but that didn't stop him from licking his fingers.

The day was the same old, same old. The only exception was that his thoughts drifted back to the hot guy at the bakery. He knew what his spank fantasies would be about that night. It wasn't like his job forced him to think. He looked at papers and entered information into the central system that the Alliance had hooked back up after the flood. If it wasn't for them, the United States would probably still be in the dark.

So he'd enter some top-secret data while picturing himself licking those tattoos. He wondered what the guy's cock looked like. Hell, he wondered what name he should be screaming.

His supervisor, Mr Jordan, walked over while he was in the middle of a daydream, his cock rock-hard in his pants while he gazed off into nothingness.

"Mr Clark, is there a problem with your computer?"

"No, sir." Rico sat up straighter.

Desk work sucked the life out of him and his boss was a prick, but he had to do something.

"Good. Back to it then." Mr Jordan clasped him on the shoulder and walked away.

With a sigh he got back to the daily grind. His dick deflated and he wanted to keep it that way until he got home. Then all bets were off.

* * * *

Walking home cooled him down somewhat. His libido under control, he started thinking about food. Of course, that brought him back to the tattooed god from that morning. Did he really want to pig out? His usual fare was a pizza, or something equally greasy. No meat, of course. Not for him — it cost too much and was hard to find. Most of the animals had become extinct and those that were left were used for eggs or milk. People had to pay top dollar for a good steak or chicken. It was getting a little better as time went on, but prices hadn't gone down much.

Or he could have ice cream. That sounded good too, with a candy topping. He had a cupboard full of cookies, his main food group. It couldn't keep up or he'd be more than a little overweight. With his sedentary lifestyle he was well on his way to being morbidly obese.

Instead of going home he headed for the nearest gym. Not his best idea on an empty stomach, but he wasn't thinking straight. If he was, he would have stopped at the store for something healthy to eat first. He was thinking that he was overweight and that he would never find a man if he felt bad about himself, so exercise would work.

Maybe he'd just sign up today and not actually do any of the work. It was a sad state of affairs that it took a hot guy to get him to this point. He had been in the Special Forces and in the top shape of his life just a few years ago. If the guys in his division could see him now, they might just cry.

This is stupid.

Rico didn't have any gym clothes. He paused at the door and watched as fit people went in and out. Why was it that he never saw overweight people going to the gym? He shut his eyes and rubbed them with his fingers. He could do this. He walked up the stairs and saw a button and a palm scanner by the door. He pushed the button and waited. There was a buzz and the door opened.

The place was set up nicely. It wasn't easy to see into the gym from the front. It was sectioned off so that when customers walked straight into a lobby they only saw the reception area and a door. That made him feel a bit more comfortable.

"Can I help you, sir?" A perky woman gave him a big smile.

"Ah—yes, I'd like to do a tour of your facilities and maybe sign up for a membership."

"Let me get one of the trainers." She winked at him. "If you'll have a seat, they'll be right with you."

Lord save him from happy-happy people. It just wasn't natural. The chair was a bit uncomfortable, but he didn't have long to wait. A woman who looked remarkably like the one at the front desk walked up to him.

"Hello! I'm Jeanne, what can I help you with today?" She held out her hand.

Rico stood and shook it. She was just as perky as the other one. What—did they clone these people? No way could they be happy and perfect. It had to be a front. He wondered what lurked underneath. He shook it off and answered.

"I'm Rico and I want to get into better shape." He stated the obvious. Why else would a fat person be at a gym? It wasn't like they had sweets. Unless that was a new form of torture where they held the candy out of reach and made people chase it.

He shuddered at the mental image of his fat ass running after a candy bar attached to a fishing pole.

"If you'll follow me." Jeanne turned and swiped her hand against an ID plate. Rico heard the clanking of weights.

They must've had stellar soundproofing. Walking in, if he hadn't known that it was a gym, he'd have had no clue. Jeanne slowed down a little until she walked beside him. She was a cute little thing. Blonde hair, blue eyes and—perfect. If he swung that way, he might've been interested, but the only thing she did was remind him of tattoos and how those arms would feel wrapped around him.

"Through there are the locker rooms. Were you planning on starting today?" Jeanne looked him up and down.

"No. Um... I just wanted to check things out first. I didn't bring any clothes and I came straight from work."

"All right, then." She clapped her hands together and continued walking. "If you sign up with us today, we're doing a special for a month's free membership. That would include the use of a personal trainer. That would be me." She turned to smile at him. He expected to see rainbows and unicorns twirling around her head at her tone, like some freaky anime. Yep, she was too chipper. "We'll probably start you off with cardio and a few light weights to help build yourself up. We don't want to go full-force right away or you'll hurt something. There are a of couple machines we'll start with. You'll change it up so your body doesn't have time to get bored. The treadmill is always popular to start off with. We also have some ellipticals and bikes. There is an indoor track. To cool down, we'll probably walk a few laps. The gym also has a hot tub, pool and sauna." Jeanne pointed things out as they moved around the room.

He wondered if her evil side would come out once they started in on the exercise. Maybe then instead of puppies and kittens he'd see horns and demon-red eyes. He really needed to stop this inner monologue on freakishly happy people. They'd walked a circle around the area and stopped by the door.

"What are your hours?"

"We're open twenty-four hours a day, seven days a week. We do a background check on all of our members and we'll get your hand scan on file. If you noticed, all the machines have a thumbprint starter. This will log in all of your information in case you come at a time when the trainers aren't available. This way we can track your improvement and make sure you're doing the exercises correctly. We run a secure place so our fees are just a bit higher, but we're totally worth it. If you'd like we can go to my office and look over the contract?"

She seemed just a tad too eager. He wondered if she was the devil in disguise and he was signing his life away, but what the hell, he was going to do this.

Well, I'm signing away my candy privileges.

He sighed and followed her into the office of doom and no more cookies.

Chapter Two

The next day Rico packed a gym bag and headed out of the door, walking his regular route to work. He passed the bakery. Rico had planned on bypassing it, he was trying to get fit…but there was the guy again. He'd dreamed about him last night, his first wet dream in a long time. He slowed to a stop and stared. The guy was wiping the counter off and his muscles were straining as he tackled a particularly stubborn stain, the tattoos flexing and moving as if they were alive. Rico licked his lips and, if he wasn't in public, he might have adjusted his cock, it was getting hard.

The blond looked up and he winked as if he knew he was being watched. Without thinking, Rico walked in. He didn't go to the counter. Instead he found a table where he could sit and watch. He ignored the calls from the owner about his usual. Sweets wouldn't cut it — unless he could lick them off that body.

"You're early today. Would you like your usual?"

Rico had to tear his gaze away. "Ah, no, not today. Do you have any…I don't know…bran muffins?"

That sounded healthy enough to him. It was a good way to start the day. He looked back over at the counter and missed what his waitress said.

"I'm sorry…what?"

"We have a banana bran muffin. It's sugar- and gluten-free."

"That's perfect."

"You want it wrapped up?"

"No, I think I'll eat it here today. I have the time."

Rico had got up early to head to the gym before work. He knew that if he waited until the end of the day that he wouldn't go. He searched around and didn't see the guy anywhere. He wondered what his name was. Maybe he should ask.

"Here's your muffin. Would you like some coffee?"

He turned in his chair and there he was. His voice honey smooth and great—now he had a boner. What had he asked? Oh—a drink.

"N-no. Green tea?"

"Coming right up."

Rico watched him walk away. He was wearing tight jeans and his ass looked biteable. Rico really needed to stop before he embarrassed himself.

It didn't take long to get the tea—Rico had just taken a bite of his muffin. It wasn't too bad, but he missed his usual treat. The man put Rico's drink on the table and sat across from Rico.

"It's my break. You don't mind if I sit here, do you?"

He didn't wait for an answer, not that Rico was in any position to say anything. All he could do was stare into the bright green eyes. He smiled at the blond.

The guy, Rico, was adorable. Not that Gilliland Carter would tell him that. He'd noticed him yesterday when he'd stopped in for a sweet. Rico was tall and had about a good two inches on Gill. He was a big guy all around and Gill wanted to snuggle him.

It had been a while since he'd felt this instant attraction and, if he wasn't mistaken, it was mutual. He needed to get his life in order first, though. No more fights over sleeping space or wondering where his next meal was going to come from. But he didn't need to think about it at that moment and stopped himself from rubbing at his black eye. He was taking his break with a cute man who he wanted to know more about. First and foremost, if he was gay and single.

Not that he'd ask just then. Maybe later. It seemed like Rico was a regular, but it looked like that might change.

He pointed to the ground by Rico's feet.

"So—I see you have a gym bag there, headed to work out?"

He missed working out. He did some modified exercises in his apartment, but there was nothing like a real gym workout.

"Ah—yeah, I just joined a place yesterday." Rico fiddled with his muffin before taking a big bite.

He licked his lips and it was all Gill could do not to groan. Fuck, he was good-looking and it had been too long since he'd been fucked. Rico looked like he could pound Gill through a mattress and still give him more.

"Good for you." Gill winked.

"Yeah—" Rico looked uncomfortable and his face went red.

Gill wasn't sure why. He hoped he hadn't done anything to offend him. Maybe he wasn't gay. It'd be just Gill's luck.

"I should go. Yes, it's time. I don't want to be late." Rico got up and hurried out of the bakery.

He wondered what that was all about. Gill shrugged and finished his coffee before cleaning up the table.

* * * *

The next two days it was the same thing. Rico would show up and sit down. Gill would join him and neither really said anything. They just relaxed until Rico would say goodbye and go about his day, leaving Gill hard and frustrated. Maybe he was working it too hard. Next time he wouldn't sit down. Make Rico come to him.

The building shook from what sounded like an explosion.

"What the hell! Ms Holly, stay here, get under the counter, I'll go see what's going on." Gill raced to the door and his heart sank. Whatever it was had caused Rico to crumble to the ground.

Not good, so very not good. He hadn't even introduced himself, going for the mystery and hoping for the best. Rico had never asked so he hadn't said anything and now he could be dead. Gill ran faster than he ever had run in his life.

Rico had reached the gym when an explosion lit up the sky. He saw it before he felt or heard it. He was on the ground, he didn't even know how he'd got there. Rubble smacked into him. He tried to get his arms over his head but he wasn't quick enough. Another round hit close to his position with smoke billowing and flames everywhere. He started coughing and had a hard time breathing. His chest was tight, but he had to remain calm or it would get worse. Stupid asthma, and he didn't have his inhaler on him. It was in his gym bag and he couldn't find the damn thing. He hoped it was still intact, but he didn't have high hopes. That kind of blast could destroy anything in its path and he just happened to be smack dab in the middle of it and not feeling too lucky.

Rico crawled away, his hands getting scraped up and bloodied from the debris on the ground, not to mention his ears echoing with the sounds of the bombs. He knew people must be screaming around him, but he had a ringing in his ears. It was total chaos, he was lucky he didn't get trampled. He had no idea where all the people came from. While he'd been walking the street had been mostly clear. More concrete from the buildings rained over and around him. Someone stumbled over him, but kept going, not even offering to help him. He was shaking and sweating, but there was nothing he could do about that now, he had to find his bag.

This was something out of one of his nightmares. What was going on? There hadn't been riots in years.

"Citizens, please return to your homes and await further instructions," a monotone voice repeated over and over again.

Where was that voice coming from? It didn't identify who was speaking. Rico didn't know if it was the Alliance or a different faction. He didn't watch the news much anymore. A drone circled the area and that must have been where the announcement was coming from.

Rico moved across the ground despite the pain in his hands, keeping himself low, his training kicking in. Another bomb exploded, leaving a crater not far from where he was. All hell was breaking loose and he needed to get away from the source. If there was such a place. It seemed like the world was ending, but his breathing was slowly returning to normal. He wouldn't need his inhaler after all. Thank goodness it wasn't a worse attack or he'd be in trouble.

Note to self, keep the damn thing in my pocket from now on.

He reached the steps and the sounds stopped. Everything was silent. It was strange how little noise there was. No birds or the normal hum of the city — the white noise most people didn't notice unless it wasn't there. But had the bombing stopped or was it the calm before the storm?

"Hey, man — you okay?"

Rico turned his head and shook it. He had to be hallucinating. The guy from the bakery was holding out a hand to help him off the ground.

"Rico. That's your name, right? Let me help you up."

He took the offer and struggled to his feet. Bakery man was stronger than he appeared.

"Yeah. That's me. Rico. Ah... How did you get here so fast?" Rico dusted himself off.

There were a few scrapes, but he wasn't hurt too seriously. His suit, on the other hand, would have to be thrown away. It was ripped in so many spots and covered in drops of blood.

"Oh, well, I heard the explosion and ran out of the shop to see what it was." Gill pointed his thumb behind him, towards the bakery. "I saw you fall and hurried over. I figured you might need the help." He shrugged like it was no big deal.

If he only knew how much Rico wanted to sex him up, he might not have been so quick to help. Hell, he might not even be gay. It would be Rico's luck.

"Well, thank you. And you are...?" Rico raised a brow.

They really didn't have time for small talk and should've been taking shelter, but for some reason he had to know this person's name. They'd been talking for a couple of days and if the world was going to end...he had to know who he'd been lusting after.

"Sorry. I'm Gilliland Carter, but most just call me Gill." Gill smiled and put his hands in his pockets, rocking back on his heels. He looked almost hesitant and Rico wanted to eat him up—with a spoon. Oh, and maybe some chocolate, covered in whipped cream.

So I'm a stress eater now, fuck.

But it did sound good and so not the point right now with the world coming down around their ears.

"Gill. Great. We need to take cover."

Something whistled through the air. Fuck, it was another bomb.

What the hell is going on?

"Hit the deck!" Gill screamed and tackled him.

"Ump." Rico smacked his back onto the ground.

Gill landed on top of him. That was too close for comfort. If Gill hadn't acted they'd both be dead, but now all he could think about was the fact that this handsome man was on top of him. Shit, he was getting hard. Talk about embarrassing. He hoped Gill didn't notice.

"You're right. We need to get out of here. It seems like this is the target zone." Gill looked down at him and Rico couldn't look away from the light green eyes. What was it about Gill that captivated him so? It could be how good he looked, but even that wasn't completely it. Gill wasn't his usual type. He liked tall, dark and hairy. Gill was none of those, but he sure was strong. His lean body hard in all the right places.

Damn it, thoughts like those weren't going to make his erection go away. Gill grinned at him. This really wasn't the time for this and another bomb exploding close to them highlighted that fact. They were going to die out there if they didn't get a move on.

Chapter Three

Gill couldn't believe that this was happening. Nothing in his training had prepared him for fuckin' bombs dropping. He'd never been military and the police department only gave a person so much training. Not that it was his job anymore. The Alliance had taken care of that. If you weren't a soldier you weren't of use to them.

Now he worked in a bakery. It was the only thing he could get because he wasn't military material with his tats and piercing and there was really no need for security, at least not that he could find. Gill wasn't a big bulky guy anyway. Most people wanted hulk-looking guys as bodyguards and that was something he'd never be. He was tired of living on the streets and a friend of a friend got him the job. Who knew what would happen now? He was afraid to look back and see if the bakery was still standing. He was living above the place and if he had to see his new home decimated it might just break him. What he didn't expect was Rico to walk into the place again that morning. Not that he should have been too surprised.

The owners did say he was a regular, but the way he kept looking at him had Gill in a constant state of arousal. It was the silver eyes that got to him. There was something in them that spoke to Gill.

And how about that? Rico was getting hard. He felt it too. He leant down and brushed his lips against Rico's and had to grin when Rico's eyes opened wide, like he couldn't believe it was happening.

"Someone's coming."

Gill blinked.

"Huh?" He pulled back and shook his head.

It was a kiss. No one got off on just a kiss. Well, he was a bit dazed from the simple lip-on-lip action and wanted to know what Rico tasted like, but nowhere near ready to shoot his load. The kiss had been good, but not spectacular. He'd have to fix that for next time. And there *would* be a next time. There had to be.

"A person. Over there." Rico jerked his head to the right and rolled over, putting Gill under him.

Man, he really was out of it. He was thinking about making out in what looked like a war zone. They hadn't had this kind of activity on Earth in—well, as long as he could remember.

"Friendly?" he whispered.

It was time to get back into the game. He had to *do* something. And not Rico, no matter how much he wanted to.

"No idea," Rico said quietly.

"Shit. I wish I had my gun."

"Bakery work that dangerous?" Rico cocked an eyebrow.

"Bakery? Oh...no, used to be a cop."

Gill couldn't see around Rico and it was like Rico was trying to protect him. It was kinda nice, not that he really needed it, gun or no gun.

"Gentlemen, you need to vacate the streets. I don't know if you've noticed, but we've got a situation going on here. We're asking anyone with fighting experience to head down to the government offices for a briefing," a gruff voice spoke above them.

Rico stood and held out a hand to help Gill up. He nodded his thanks and brushed himself off. The man in uniform looked menacing with his riot gear on, his hand hovering over his gun. Like they were going to jump him or something. Gill almost snorted.

"Sir, what's going on here?" Rico asked.

"I have no idea. I was just told to gather any fighters and send the others to a few secure locations around town."

"Thank you. You said go to the government offices. Will they know what's going on?" Rico was taking charge of the conversation.

He was different now than he was in the bakery or even a few seconds ago. There was an air about him that made Gill even harder, if that was possible.

"Why don't you head down to the shelter on Main? Your friend there should head on over to the offices."

Rico drew up tall and his face got hard, his eyes went dark. Gill licked his lips. This dominant side of Rico was a real turn-on. He pictured being held down tight and fucked hard.

"I suggest you don't worry about me and be about your business. Now, I'll ask again, the government offices, right?"

"Yes, sir." The soldier gulped.

Rico nodded and turned on his heel. Gill followed.

He looked around him. The whole area was demolished. Fires were burning all over the place. Sirens rang in the distance, screeching, with the drones in the background blaring their updates.

There were a few people who staggered around, looking dazed. Most of them were hustling out of the city with panic clearly written in their body language. A kid screamed and tears streaked down his chubby cheeks, leaving black marks streaking his dirty face. No one looked too badly hurt. Not that his rudimentary first-aid skills would really help anyone who was seriously injured. Rico had got ahead of him, with his long strides. Gill hurried to catch up.

"That was impressive." Gill patted Rico on his back.

And it was. The way Rico had stood up to the soldier had been amazing, but out of the corner of his eye he saw another transformation. Rico sort of…deflated.

"Yeah, I might be fat, but I'm not useless."

"Fat?" Gill was bewildered.

"Like you didn't notice." Rico smoothed his hand over his stomach.

Gill took a really good look at Rico. He was taller than Gill by a couple of inches and he had a big build on him. Dark brown hair with those silver eyes. He was wearing a suit, not the most flattering outfit for him, and, sure, he might have a few pounds on him, but he didn't look bad.

"Look good to me." Gill shrugged.

Rico looked at him like he was nuts. "Right."

"It's all superficial and I'm not about that. But, dude, you're wearing a suit. Are you sure about fighting? Maybe—"

Rico's glare stopped anything Gill might have said.

"I was in the military, I know my way around a gun. It might have been a few years ago, but some things you don't forget."

"You were made to lead," Gill agreed. He'd bet Rico had been high-ranking when he was in the services. It would have been hot to see him in his day, but no hotter than Rico was right now, though Gill didn't think Rico would believe him.

"You don't even know me. How can you say that?" Rico shoved his hands into his pockets in a defensive pose.

"You stared that guy down and told him who was boss. It wasn't just your tone, it was your body language, and fuck if it wasn't hot."

Gill couldn't believe he'd said that out loud, but it was true and he wouldn't take the words back now.

"You think *I'm* hot?" There was that disbelief again. He wondered what he'd have to do to convince Rico he was attractive.

I don't know, but I bet it'd be fun to find out.

They'd reached the building. It looked a little rough around the edges, but it was still standing. Men and woman were filing in. Gill and Rico got in line.

He moved closer to Rico and stood on tiptoes to get to his ear. "Yes, you're hot and if whatever is going on here wasn't happening I'd take you home and let you fuck my brains out. Why do you think I kept sitting with you? I wanted to get to know you more. I've been hot for you from the first moment I saw you come into the bakery."

A slow red spread over Rico's face. It was cute and Gill wanted to explore it—see if it was as warm as it looked. It sucked that the timing was so off. If it had held off a couple days he probably could have had Rico in his bed.

Rico cleared his throat, but didn't say anything. Gill wanted to see how far he could push it, but they were getting closer to the door. A guard stood with his arms crossed over his chest. They were stopping people and asking questions before they let them in.

"Name and background."

"Ricardo Clark. I served five years in the Army. My MOS when I was discharged was Special Forces Assistant Operations and Intelligence."

Gill did a double-take and so did the officer standing there. Special Forces? *No fucking way.*

They let Rico go through and it was his turn.

"Gilliland Carter. I was an undercover detective on the police force until Alliance shut us down. Served for over ten years."

They let him in too and he rushed forward to see where Rico had gone. He hadn't gone far.

"Special Forces?"

"Well, it's been a few years, but yeah." Rico looked embarrassed, not that he had any reason to be.

"I never would have guessed."

"The fat thing, right?"

"You need to get over that. No, the baby face thing. Or maybe it was the suit. You look more like an office drone." Gill grinned, wanting Rico to know he was teasing.

"I was medically discharged, okay? They were looking for people to get rid of and I wasn't going to fight it. I developed asthma."

"They could have totally controlled that." Now Gill was starting to get upset on Rico's behalf, even if it had happened years ago. What a bunch of bunk.

"They could have, but I took the out. There were others who had families to support." Rico shrugged.

So not only was he sexy and strong, he was honourable. It would take years for Gill to fully understand every facet of Rico and it might be worth it. Why couldn't he have met him before?

Gill didn't leave Rico's side, but he took a good look around at the building they were in. It was a government building with one of those big entranceways. There weren't too many people milling around, which didn't bode well if they were going to have to go to war. It looked like a couple of them were even injured. As a whole, the group looked a bit dejected. That wasn't a way to go into a war. At least he didn't think so.

It had been years since they had experienced anything like exploding buildings and violence. They had all become complacent as peace had settled over the world. They should have known that something was going to happen to wreck their utopia.

Isn't that how it always works?

Not that he saw much of that in his life, but, as a majority, the people did.

Maybe it was him, but everyone looked so young. Where were all the hardened, seasoned men and women of the old armed forces?

Hopefully, they had already been deployed. If not, they might be screwed.

They milled around for a few minutes before someone with a microphone began to speak. Rico moved closer and Gill followed. He wasn't ready to let him out of his sight yet.

"By now all of you are aware that something is going on. We are under attack. They have hit military bases all over the planet and we've lost some great men today. We need every available fighting man and woman we can find. A military background is a plus because we don't have a lot of time to train. We're going to strike back and strike back hard. As of now they haven't made any demands and we are unsure of who is targeting us. We are starting to believe it might be first contact with an outside source." There was a muffled sound and the high screech of the feedback from the microphone and a "What the fuck?" that Gill was sure they weren't meant to hear.

It was pandemonium after that. People were being sectioned into different groups. He knew the separation was coming and was upset. Rico went one way and he went another. Rico looked back, regret showing all over his face. Gill closed his eyes and pinched his nose.

Fuck.

The timing sucked, and timing was everything. If he'd tried a little harder they could have at least had a more intimate connection before they'd been forced apart. He opened his eyes and lifted a hand in farewell. Rico returned the gesture before heading towards the group they ushered him into. They might never see each other again and it shouldn't hurt, because they'd just met, but for some reason he felt like his future had just walked away from him.

Gill shook his head to rid himself of the haunting feeling and he paid attention to the officer in front of him. They were going to get a crash course in military protocol, then they were headed to D.C. Something about swearing in and making things official before going to a base. More quick training to brush up any skills they possessed. He was going to be a grunt. Something he'd never expected, but he guessed his appearance didn't matter when the world was coming crashing down around them.

Chapter Four

"Hit them again, Colonel?"

"No, I think that is enough of a show of force. I want to be patched through to the leader down there ASAP."

"Yes, sir." The Lieutenant turned and worked on the comms.

Colonel Scott Winchester surveyed his ship. He couldn't believe the intel he'd received. It had taken a while to reach him out in space and he still had a few contacts on Earth. The news was disturbing to say the least. Someone had overthrown the United States of America. The President was no more and everything he'd believed in was gone. He wouldn't have it. Someone had to take a stand and it might as well be him.

The crews hadn't been gone that long. A decade at most. When he'd found out what was going on he'd hurried back, putting out the call to all of the other ships to come home. It was time.

His mission was to explore space and see what was in the galaxy, maybe even beyond. The government had always had a fascination with what was out there. When the scientists had finally found a way to conduct stable space jumps, they'd sent twenty spaceships in to space with full crews to find out what was there and if there were any other viable planets they could inhabit if the need ever arose.

The things he'd found were amazing and now he had no one to share them with.

One of the most interesting things he'd found was that most of the other species were humanoid. No little green men like people thought. No squat brown things like that kids' movie he couldn't remember the name of. Sure, there were some differences, like the one race that had gills so they could swim underwater. Most of their planet was ocean. Scott had planned to visit there with his wife until he'd got the call that he was needed back home.

The ships they'd had were so much better and his ship had received upgrades because of it. The warp capability was out of this world, literally. Earth was a baby compared to some of the worlds he'd visited. The best thing was the translator. Once it was embedded in a person's ear they could communicate with any species.

Now he had to deal with something called the Alliance, which had taken over. He didn't have anyone to report to. Even the military was different from what he'd heard. Now he was the highest-ranking officer left and he had to take responsibility for the others. They all looked to him. It had taken a bit of wrangling to get all the ships gathered, but now they were strategically placed around the globe. Some of them hadn't wanted to come but Scott had convinced them. The wonders of the universe pulled them all, but first they needed to take care of matters at home.

Maybe he should have talked first, but he had no idea how combative the Alliance would be and a show of force always worked best in these kinds of situation, to let them know he meant business. Next would be the ground troops. His contact had them waiting to go, but first he wanted to talk to these people. His contact on Earth had made it seem like war would be the only way to get America back to its former self.

"Sir, they're online."

"This is Commandant Walker. Identify yourself."

The audacity of the man, demanding he do anything. Scott was in charge of this conversation.

"You really don't have the authority to command me to do anything, Commandant."

Had the Russians taken over? What was with the Commandant? That couldn't be it. When he'd left things had been friendly between the countries. Hell, even the Middle East had settled down. Had they invaded? America's forces were stronger than that and his contact hadn't said anything about a nuclear strike, only that the world tended to listen when the Alliance spoke.

"I am with the Alliance. What or who are you?"

"I am the person who is taking your terrorist organisation down and bringing the United States of America back to its former glory. Surrender now and we'll go easy on you."

"Again—who are you and what do you want?"

"I am Colonel Scott Winchester of the United States Air Force and you will stand down."

"There is no Air Force anymore. Just the Alliance. It's you who needs to stand down. Call back your ships or we will open fire."

"I'll call your bluff. The vast majority of your ships are down. Next to go will be your lines of communication. I'm sending a battalion to your capital and you'll turn yourselves over to them. I'm instating martial law until a new President can be elected."

Scott turned off the comms. It was getting him nowhere. He'd have to go forward with his threat.

"Lieutenant, get a hold of Captain Samms and patch him through to my room. Take evasive manoeuvres for any incoming missiles. I want to be made aware if anything big heads our way. Alert the others to be on standby. I want reports from the ships hovering over the other countries. Be prepared for war, gentlemen."

He left the bridge and headed for his room. This might be his last chance for some downtime before this crazy thing was over. It might be years, but he was ready for it. No one would take away the freedom he'd grown up with.

"How did it go?"

Nancy, his wife, sat on the bed. He'd tried to convince her to stay on Alto, one of the planets they had discovered, but she'd refused, wanting to be with him instead, saying she didn't want to wait to hear what happened.

"It's as we expected. The Alliance has taken over and has refused to surrender." He took off his shirt and put it on the chair. He needed a shower.

"Are you sure about this? They might not be hostile."

"They overthrew the President." *Why can't she understand the importance of that?*

"But how do you know? You're taking the word of someone you haven't seen in over ten years. Maybe we should go down and take a look. See what's going on."

"Honey, we don't know the whole situation down there, but they won't stand down."

"Would you?"

"What do you mean?" He turned to look at her.

"If you were in charge of the world and you had ships surrounding it, coming from out of the blue, would you just give up? You did go in hot. I told you to talk to them first."

"I know. I know. But this was the best way."

"I still think we—"

"It'll be okay."

"You just declared war, didn't you?" She got off the bed and wrapped her arms around him.

"I did."

"Then it won't be okay for a very long time. We should have stayed on Alto. We had a good life there."

"But this is home we're talking about."

"No—it isn't. Not anymore. Home is Alto. We could have been happy there." She kissed his shoulder.

"What about kids?"

"What about them?"

"When we have them, don't you want to bring them to Earth so they can see where they come from?"

"We're their beginnings, not some planet we haven't seen in a very long time."

"It's a matter of honour."

Nancy snorted. "You call it what you will, but we were happy. So were the others. And who knows? We could have visited if you'd gone in with a calm head and talked to them."

"No more arguing, okay? What's done is done. Let's just live through this."

"I want to go back, when this is over." Nancy stroked a hand down his shoulder and gave it a kiss.

"Whatever you want, honey." Scott patted her hand. "I'm going to go shower and take a short nap. Let me know when the reports start coming in."

She let go of him and he finished undressing.

"Yes, sir." She saluted him.

Scott grinned and smacked her ass. In a way he was happy that she was with him. They might fight, but he'd need her strength in the days to come. He couldn't question his decisions. Not now. His path was started and he would follow it through to the bitter end.

Chapter Five

A year later...

"Captain Clark, your orders, sir?"

Rico still couldn't get over the fact that he was back in the military and fighting in a war that should have never been. The whole world was up in arms, literally. The forces against them were relentless, and neither the Alliance nor the Old Guard wanted to give in. There were too many casualties on both sides. The Alliance hadn't expected the invaders to have ground forces and hadn't taken precautions. Its focus was wholly on the air raids.

It amazed the hell out of him that he was piloting his own ship as well, the *Annihilation*. Sweet name for a warship. He would've rather been on the ground, but the war wouldn't be won there. The greater part of the fighter force was in the sky. Their ships were too powerful and the Alliance didn't have any heavy-duty ships at its disposal. They'd all been destroyed in the first wave of attacks. It had taken months for Rico to get back into fighting shape, but he was happier now than he'd been in a long time.

"Get some rest, Corporal. You're going to need it."

"Yes, sir."

They had a pickup scheduled for the next day. A group of troops was being transferred to his ship and there was a mission planned. He didn't know all of the details. He was to be fully briefed by the soldier in charge.

The Alliance had picked up one of the Old Guard, as it had taken to calling the insurgents, and had been told of the exploration the President had started before the flood. The group hadn't been heard from in a long time and was thought to have been lost.

Who knew they'd come back and try to re-establish America the way it was before they'd left, not giving the Alliance a chance to let them know it wasn't a hostile takeover? The Alliance wanted to know more about the planets that had been found and the technology of the ships that the Old Guard had arrived in. He did know it was going to be the troops' job to infiltrate the main ship and find the coordinates for the other planets. If they managed to take over the ship, even better so the Alliance could get its technicians to look at the schematics of the engine and the weapons. Their technology was beyond anything Rico had ever seen.

What they had now wouldn't give them interstellar travel. He was lucky his ship could even get into space at all. As it was, he had to have two engineers working around the clock to keep her running. She needed a complete overhaul, but there hadn't been time. The technology they needed was buried in un-entered data. Things that had been lost in the flood. The

Alliance was freaking out trying to find what it needed as fast as it could.

Rico had scheduled downtime in a few weeks, but who knew if he and the ship would actually get it.

He thought back to that day a year ago when this whole thing had started. A lot had happened in those first few days. He'd got his self-respect back and was really living for the first time since being discharged from the Special Forces. He was in his element. Some days he even remembered Gill. He wondered what had happened to him. He'd probably never know now. The baker-ex-cop could be dead for all he knew. It was silly to miss someone who he didn't really know, but they'd had a connection. At least there had been one on his end and it had seemed to be the same for Gill.

If they'd had a chance to develop something it would have made the separation all the harder. He should be thankful he hadn't really got to know Gill.

There was no time for personal business anyway. It was best to forget things that he couldn't change. He sighed at the memory of Gill's face and shook off thoughts of the other man. He punched in the coordinates to the drop spot. The troops wouldn't be there until morning, but they had the time. The ship hummed to life and went on its merry way.

"You should get some rest as well."

He turned to see his second-in-command standing behind his chair.

"I will. I just wanted to get the ship moving."

"I could have done that, sir."

"I know."

"You just like to be in command."

Funny how that statement took him back, once again, to that day a year ago.

"I won't deny that. So, tomorrow we'll pick up the troops. I'm not sure what the mission will involve after that, just that they need to get close to the main ship. Their Captain is supposed to report to me first thing and brief me. When we're done, I'll get you the coordinates and we'll get back landside."

"Good, the men need a break from space. They're starting to get cranky."

"They'd better get used to it. If things go well, we'll be exploring space for years at a time. The Alliance wants to take over where the President and his administration left off. If we can't get the Old Guard to join us, we're going to take control ourselves."

"Are you sure about this?"

"We don't have a choice. Not with the way this war is going. Earth is on its last legs. The drafts have started and no one thought that would be possible after all the flooding. And the bombs the Old Guard are using have destroyed a lot of the atmosphere. Soon it won't be able to sustain us. We need to find new planets and, if the detainee is right, there are places out there we can settle on."

"I know. It just doesn't seem right."

"I hear you. We'll try to do it peacefully, but I'm not above a hostile takeover."

"Yes, sir." Manny squeezed his shoulder.

And he wasn't. Rico would do whatever necessary to make sure the people on that planet were safe. They didn't start this and he wasn't going to let them die for a war the Old Guard started. They had already lost too many men. He really hoped the overthrow wouldn't have to happen. The Old Guard had lost just as many people over something that was senseless.

"Now prepare the crew for tomorrow. I'll be in the mess hall, then the gym if you need me."

"Aye-aye, Captain."

He got out of the chair and stretched out the kink in his back. He didn't mind being in space like some of the men, but he'd be happy to be on solid ground again. The mess hall wasn't far from the bridge. Men and woman were in and out at all hours. The food wasn't too bad, but some days he missed his pastries. No more of those for him, though. He needed to keep in fighting shape.

"What can we get for you today, Captain?" one of the cooks asked.

Most ships had AI doing the cooking and such tasks, but Rico liked the human touch and kept his ship staffed with real people. They needed jobs. Hell, everyone needed something. People were starving down on Earth. If he had the chance he'd cold-cock the man who'd started this and try to wake him up to what he was doing.

Earth had been peaceful for the first time in a really long time, thanks to the Alliance, and the Old Guard had destroyed that.

"Something light, I'm going for a workout after."

"Yes, sir." She handed him a protein shake and a salad.

That would do. He went to his table. He thought it was silly to have a whole table to himself, but the crew had insisted. No one ever sat there but him. He wasn't above these people, no matter what his rank said.

He finished up his meal and headed for the gym. It was his second home while on the ship. Most of his free time was spent there. This was how he should have spent his free moments after he was discharged the first go-round, but it was useless to think of woulda, shoulda, coulda.

Tomorrow was going to be a test for everyone. He didn't know the intricate details of the mission, but he did know they were going to try to take over the main ship. They'd tried in the past and it hadn't ended well. One of their ships had approached one of the Old Guard vessels and it had been shot blown to bits as soon as it had got within firing distance, and those ships had a long reach. The Alliance was getting desperate, but he didn't know how this time would be different. He'd have to make it so because he wasn't losing a single member of his crew.

Not that Rico blamed them. People were dying. The planet was dying. Something big had to be done.

He wanted to know why this Scott Winchester wasn't talking. The guy was dead-set on things being his way, not listening to the fact that things had been better before he'd come back. The Alliance wasn't taking away human rights. Not really. It just made the big decisions without all the wait and hassle the old system had had. Sure, it wasn't the be-all and end-all, but it was working. If not for them, after the President, the Vice President, most of the Senate and Cabinet were all gone, then it would have been total chaos if someone hadn't stepped up. The tragedy of that day would be forever etched in the lives of those who were there.

Rico got on the treadmill and zoned out while he ran. It gave him more time to think of things that he didn't want to remember. The images of people screaming as the flood overtook them, the scramble for higher ground. Knowing that others were trapped and there was nothing anyone could do about it.

The government had tried to secure the Executive Office to no avail. They'd been caught in a surge of water and dragged under. A few others had been locked away for safety and then trapped inside their 'safe' homes. After the flood had receded the military had gone in to open up the places only to find everyone inside dead. There had been a faulty seal that had allowed the floodwaters to rush into the space. It wasn't like they'd had anywhere else to go. They'd been trapped like rats in a ship and bodies littered the place. The pictures had been devastating with bloated corpses everywhere. It was an image that would never leave him no matter how hard he tried to forget.

God, he really didn't want to think about that. He upped the speed and difficulty on the machine and ran harder. It was time to get away from all these morbid thoughts. Instead he'd think about the man he'd left behind. The one he'd felt a connection with. Gill.

Rico smiled remembering the tatted-up, pierced man. He knew what those arms felt like around him since Gill had saved his life. Now he pictured the both of them in a bedroom, naked. Rico wondered if there were tattoos anywhere else on Gill's body. It was sad that his jerk-off material was a man he didn't even really know, but Gill was forever in his mind. Possibly because he was the one who'd got away.

Of course, it was the wrong time to be fantasising about Gill. A hard-on in the gym, one that he couldn't take care of, could be painful. Instead, he cleared his mind and went to his happy place, where the Earth had been beautiful and rich, full of life. A day at the beach with the water lapping gently on the shore. Rico's breathing calmed and he could hear the steady thump of his feet as he ran and ran. The treadmill beeped at him before he was ready. He stumbled a little as it turned off. He'd do his weights tomorrow.

Rico cleaned off the machine and headed for his room. He'd shower there. There was too big of a chance he'd be sporting wood before the shower was over and, as much as he liked his crew, that was private.

He put his palm on the reader to open his door. It swooshed, allowing him to enter, and snapped closed behind him. He tossed his towel and clothes to the floor.

"Shower on, eighty degrees, please." The nice thing was that his shower was voice-activated. No more messing around with getting the temperature right — the computer did it all for him.

Rico put his hands on the wall and let the hot water beat on his muscles, relaxing him. He closed his eyes and went back to his thoughts of Gill. He was alone now, in the shower. He fused Gill and the beach scene.

They were both on a towel in the sand. Gill was naked and his lean body all stretched out for him. Rico turned and just stared at all that skin on display. Gill was magnificent. Rico leaned over and traced the closest tattoos with his tongue. Gill squirmed, but didn't move. They'd done this before — Rico testing Gill's control — it was one of their favourite games. Rico reached the inside of Gill's elbow. It was one of his hot spots. They'd found it by accident the last time they'd played. He laved it, but wasn't ready to break Gill yet so he continued up the arm until he reached the wrist, another great spot, but he kept going until he could suck Gill's fingers into his mouth.

Rico moaned around the digits. Gill had Rico's cock in his hand.

Rico gripped his own cock hard, the way he liked it and stroked it, the water still beating down on him.

He arched up into that palm, his heels digging into the towel, but didn't stop sucking. Not yet, he wanted those fingers nice and wet. Finally he released them. Gill was going to come first, he'd see to that.

"Open yourself up for me, Gill."

It was Gill's turn to moan. He let go of Rico's cock to grab at his own ass. It was one of Rico's kinks to watch Gill stretch himself. It got him hotter than anything else watching those fingers go in and out of Gill's ass knowing his cock would be there soon. He didn't know where to look. He started with Gill's face. His eyes were closed in bliss and he licked his lips. Rico wanted to taste him. He raised himself over Gill's body with his hands on either side of Gill's head, not touching him anywhere, but his mouth. He nibbled his lips and waited for Gill to let him in. He ran his tongue over the seam of Gill's lips, but didn't force his way inside. Finally, Gill parted his mouth and Rico dived in, taking Gill in a forceful kiss, showing Gill how fast and hard it was going to be this time. He wasn't going to be gentle. He wanted to lay his body over Gill's, pressing him into the sand, but not yet. There was still time to drive Gill insane, if he could slow down.

He released Gill and sucked on his neck, bringing up a mark and scraping it with his teeth. As much as he wanted to slowly work his way down Gill's body, it wasn't going to happen, he was fooling himself to think it was. Rico was too turned on and wanted to be inside Gill's body. Rico pushed Gill's legs up so he could watch Gill fuck himself with his fingers.

"Mmmm – so pretty, Gill," he murmured against Gill's thigh. Maybe he could take his time with this part.

Rico licked around Gill's fingers as they plunged into his ass. "Rico – you're gonna make me come."

He wasn't ready for that. Gill couldn't come until he was inside him, but he didn't want to stop yet. Gill tasted great. Rico reached to squeeze Gill's cock at the base and gave his balls a light pinch. Gill faltered a little, but kept pumping away.

"Spread 'em." Rico didn't have to explain himself anymore than that.

Gill removed his fingers and, before he could obey Rico's command, Rico sucked on those fingers that tasted of his lover and almost came himself. Fuck – Gill was so hot.

"Rico – please."

He nodded and let go of Gill's hands. He spread his cheeks wide and Rico paused to take in the pretty picture before he got into position. Gill rested his feet on Rico's shoulders. Rico kissed Gill's foot and eased his way inside Gill's body at the same time.

"Harder, Rico," Gill panted.

Rico didn't listen. He moved back out and in an inch at a time. He wiped at the sweat streaming down his face, but refused to hurry.

Gill was whimpering and begging him to go faster, wiggling his hips. Rico pressed Gill down into the sand, gripping his hips tight, and finally gave into Gill's wishes. He snapped his hips harder and harder, losing control.

Rico stroked his hand faster and faster along his cock, the images too strong and real. What he wouldn't give to make them come alive. His balls drew up tight and he grunted as he came all over the wall.

Each fantasy was hotter than the last, but not as satisfying as the real thing. He didn't really know what Gill looked like without clothes. He sighed and got out of the shower.

"Water off."

Now he had time on his hands and he was feeling down. Maybe he'd go back to the gym and do his weights tonight instead of waiting. It would stop him from eating himself better and he'd tire himself out so that, maybe, he wouldn't dream tonight about light green eyes looking down at him with love.

Chapter Six

Gill looked at the ship, waiting for permission to dock his skimmer. The *Annihilation*. What a name for a ship. Of course, if he had to be on one, a badass one would do. He hoped they could annihilate the enemy. He was tired of this war. Tired of being in service to the Alliance.

Not that he could just up and quit. There was too much at stake. The world was crumbling around them. The only good thing that had come out of the turmoil was that the Alliance had united the entire planet, becoming the governing body of the world. The Middle East, Asia, the Russians—hell, everybody—had joined to help stop the Old Guard. Now they needed to convince the Old Guard to join as well so they could save the population from becoming extinct.

That was his job today. Not one he relished, but it had to be done. The war had gone on for too long. The end had to be now or he'd die trying.

"Captain Carter, please follow me to the ready room. We have it set up for your briefing with the Captain."

Gill looked at the man in front of him. He was hot, if a little young and small. The doors opened and Gill stopped in his tracks. His second-in-command stumbled into him.

No way in hell. It couldn't be possible. It *shouldn't* be possible. Not after all this time. He pinched himself. Nope, he wasn't dreaming.

Ricardo Clark stood beside the window. The man who had a standing invitation to his fantasies. But he looked different, harder than he had the last time they'd met.

"Captain Clark, the troops are here."

Gill stood still and waited to see if Rico recognised him. He gulped, afraid he hadn't been memorable enough. Their encounter had been so brief.

Rico turned and his eyes widened, letting him know that he shouldn't have worried about being unmemorable, if that look was anything to go by.

"Leave us," Rico said to the young man as he waved him away. Gill had forgotten about the guy the moment he'd seen Rico.

The authority in that voice made Gill's cock hard. Once again it was the wrong time. Would it ever be right?

"Captain?" the little twink officer questioned.

"You heard me. Leave me and…"

"Captain," Gill filled in.

"Yes, Captain Carter alone. Shut the door on your way out."

"Carter?" Slone, his second-in-command, questioned.

"It's okay, Slone. We'll meet up when the briefing is done. I'll find you."

Slone nodded and left the room. The only sound was the click of the door as it swept shut.

"Computer, lock the door and turn off comms unless an emergency comes up."

"Authorisation code, sir."

"Romeo-Charlie-Six-Two-Two."

"Complying."

Rico had never taken his eyes off Gill. Fuck. Rico had got even hotter over the year. His body looked to be in tip-top shape. Not that it was bad before. God, he wanted to see Rico naked. He didn't have long to wait. Rico hadn't spoken a word, but started taking off his uniform shirt. Gill was in the same position as before — beside the door, unmoving and watching.

He swallowed as each inch of Rico was revealed. He had cut abs and a trail of dark hair that disappeared into his pants. Then those came off and there was the cock he'd wondered about. It was hard already and thick. Gill's ass twitched. They had things to talk about. Important things, but he couldn't bring himself to stop Rico.

"Get out of those clothes and on the table."

Gill was well and truly fucked. Well, not yet, but it looked like it was soon to come to pass. How many times had he dreamed of this meeting? Seeing Rico again. Some of them even started this way.

"Rico—"

"Now. Unless you don't want me as much as I want you."

He scrambled out of his clothes. He wanted this. Tomorrow they might all be dead. The mission they were going on had a forty-five per cent success rate.

"We should…" He tried one more time, but his actions didn't help. He was already crawling onto the table, his ass towards Rico. He needed this too bad. It had been too long and he wasn't missing this opportunity.

"Yes, we should, but later. I've waited a year for this. I can't wait any longer."

Gill looked over his shoulder. Rico had moved closer.

"Me too," he whispered.

"Turn over." Rico slapped his ass and Gill's cock got harder and it fuckin' hurt.

Rico's silver eyes were dark with lust. His gaze trailed down Gill's body. It was almost like a touch. He wanted Rico's hand on him, more than that tap on his ass.

"Gill, tell me this isn't a dream. If it is, I don't want to wake up."

Finally, Rico trailed his fingers down Gill's body.

"If it is, we're sharing it. I need more. I ache, Rico."

"I didn't think we'd ever be here. God, you're fuckin' gorgeous. Even better than I imagined. I wondered if you had tats everywhere, but you don't—just your arms and fuck if that isn't hot. I want to lick them, worship them. Shit, I don't know where to start there's so much…"

"Press your body to mine. Please, I need to feel you everywhere. I'll beg if I have to."

"No need to beg." Rico ran his fingers down Gill's face.

"Will the table hold?" Not that he really cared. He wouldn't stop Rico if the damn thing collapsed. He wanted that thick cock up his ass.

"Guess we'll find out." Rico climbed on and Gill scooted up and turned so he was stretched out.

Rico climbed over him and slowly pressed his body against Gill's. Gill closed his eyes, the sensation overwhelming. But then Rico rocked his hips, their cocks brushed against each other.

"I need you inside me."

"It's going to be hard and fast. I don't think this first time can be any other way. I've waited too long." Rico rested his forehead on Gill's.

"Just do it." Gill moved up so he could brush their lips together.

Rico wasn't the only one who'd waited. Gill hadn't thought this moment would ever come outside of his fantasies.

"I'm not going to hurt you," Rico whispered against Gill's mouth.

"It hurts now." Gill hoped he didn't look as pathetic as he sounded. Rico had told him not to beg, but he might not be able to help himself if they didn't hurry this along.

"You up on your vaccines?"

"You know it. You?"

"Yes."

"That's good. Good. Shit, don't suppose you have any lube?"

From now on he'd carry some in his pocket—never leave his room without it, but, lube or no lube, they were doing this. Now.

"No." Rico closed his eyes.

"No worries." Gill put his fingers up to Rico's mouth.

Rico had to get off him so Gill could reach his ass.

"I've fantasised about you stretching yourself for me. God, just last night I had you spread out like this and… I'll show you. Fuck yourself with your fingers."

Rico ran his hands down Gill's thighs and held them up, almost bending Gill in half.

He didn't care and reached around, his fingers jabbing inside. It burned, but he didn't care. He was going to have Rico inside him and it was worth a bit of pain. He had to ease his finger in past the second ring of muscle, but finally it was in. He watched Rico watch him. Rico's eyes never leaving Gill's ass. It was so hot.

When Rico leant down, Gill had to squeeze his cock hard. He couldn't come until Rico was inside him, but it was going to be close. Rico was licking his ass and fingers.

"Rico. Fuck… I'm gonna… You gotta… Oh my God. Rico!"

His hand hurt from clenching his dick so hard. He almost lost it when Rico added his thumb to the equation.

"I'm going to fuck you now, Gill." Rico moved and rested Gill's thighs on his shoulders, moving him so he could reach Gill's lips.

He could taste himself on Rico. He moaned into Rico's mouth and then groaned when that thick cock slowly opened his body.

"You okay?" Rico paused.

Gill couldn't have that. He wiggled so he could grab Rico's hips and pull him closer.

"Fuck. Me," Gill panted.

He thrust in hard. Gill grunted and held on for the ride. He couldn't reach his dick, not with the way Rico had him bent, but he wasn't going to need the extra stimulation. Rico was pounding his gland with every thrust. Gill wasn't going to last.

"I'm close, Gill." Rico wiped the sweat off his forehead. He was breathing hard.

"Harder, Rico."

Rico braced his hands on the table and slammed in hard, his rhythm faltering. Gill clenched his ass. Rico threw his head back and screamed.

"Gill!"

That was all it took for Gill. His cum coated both of their stomachs. He'd never come so hard in his life. Rico collapsed on top of him. Both of them panting hard. It took a couple of minutes for Gill to come down from his orgasm. He wrapped his arms around Rico and stroked his back.

"We have things to talk about." Rico sighed.

Gill knew it. They both did, but he didn't want this moment to end yet.

"I know." Gill squeezed tight and released Rico.

He watched Rico walk naked to a sink in the back of the room. Wasn't that handy? There were glasses and other things lined up on the back counter. Rico came back with a towel and wiped them both down before handing Gill his clothes.

"Fuck, I don't want this to end, Gill." Rico ran a hand down his face.

"I don't either, but we have a war to finish."

"I should call the others back." Rico sounded resigned.

He knew just how he felt.

"You should, but you don't have to. We can confer first and then let the others know."

"Agreed. I still want a few more minutes with just the two of us."

"Me too." Gill held out his hand and Rico helped him off the table.

They both dressed and, instead of going to the chairs, Rico directed him to a bench beneath the back window. He pulled Gill close to him and wrapped him in his arms.

"What's the mission? I know we're supposed to infiltrate the enemy and try to talk some sense into them, face to face. But how?"

"The scientists came up with some sort of cloaking device. It's only worked on small things so far. I have a suit made of the stuff. You just need to get me close enough and distract them so I can board. I'm going to seek out the Colonel and talk to him. I have some data to show him that will hopefully end this whole thing."

"You can't go by yourself," Rico stated.

Like he wanted to, especially now, but he couldn't foist this off on one of his underlings. It was too dangerous and he had trained for this.

"I volunteered." Gill leaned his head back against Rico's shoulder.

"That was stupid. I just found you. I'm not losing you again." Rico held him tighter.

"We don't have a choice right now. We have to do this. If we don't, everyone below could die. We need to start transferring them to other planets as soon as possible. We need to contact other solar systems to see if we can join if they have a coalition like the Alliance."

"Fuck, Gill." Rico stroked Gill's arm.

It was comforting in a way he hadn't experienced in a really long time and hadn't thought he'd ever have with Rico.

"Shit, Rico, if I'd known..." Gill nuzzled his face into Rico's neck.

"I might not know you too well, but you would have done this anyway, wouldn't you?"

He grinned against Rico's skin. It was true and said something—that Rico could understand that when they'd only had a brief period together.

"Yes, but I wish we had more time. This could be a one-way mission. We both know it." Gill sighed.

It hadn't been a big deal before now, but he'd just found Rico again. The situation totally sucked.

"I'm going with you." Rico tangled his fingers in Gill's hair and kissed his head.

"You can't. There's only one suit."

"There has to be a way." Rico tugged at Gill's hair.

He moved so he could look into Rico's eyes.

"No time. We have to make this go down today."

Gill hated the look of sadness he'd put in Rico's eyes.

"But—"

He shook his head.

"We don't have to go right now. We could brief both of our staffs and then go back to your quarters." That was the best Gill had to offer right now.

Rico let out a heavy sigh. Gill hated that he was right, but he wanted just one more time with Rico. It could be the last.

"All right. I'll call them in. You ready?"

"As I'll ever be."

Chapter Seven

Rico couldn't believe his fucking luck. The man he'd held in his thoughts for a year was here and now he was going to lose him. Forever. Unless they could convince Colonel Winchester to stop the war, to join the Alliance and save Earth.

Sure, give them something easy. Gill looked so calm sitting at the end of the conference table. The others had no idea that just moments ago he'd fucked Gill on that surface and enjoyed every stolen second of it.

"Tonight we'll head to the space surrounding the *USS Franklin* and stop just inside of their field. Once we are on their sensors, there will be fire. The *Annihilation* will give me cover as I make my way to their ship."

"How are you going to get inside?" Rico's second-in-command wanted to know.

That was a good question and Rico waited to hear the answer. He wanted the meeting to be over. One taste of Gill wasn't enough and the next one... He couldn't think about that. Not now. He'd enjoy the moment.

"When I attach myself to their ship it should send a signal that they have a malfunction. They'll send someone to investigate. I'll have to overpower them and get inside."

"Won't that be difficult in your suit?" Again, Manny was asking the good question. One he couldn't voice for fear he'd break down.

No way could he do that. He was in charge and they expected him to always be in control. There'd be time for that later. After the mission was complete.

"Yes, but not impossible. I've been training for different contingencies." Gill let them know.

"Won't they shoot on sight once you're on board?" That came from Gill's group.

"They have a big crew, they might not notice right away. I have enough hand-to-hand combat skills. I should be fine. Plus, they won't be expecting it."

"They will be on high alert for something, though. It's been months since the Alliance has sent an actual attack on the *Franklin*. And if you're captured?" Rico hoped no one noticed the crack in his voice.

No word had come down that the crew of the *Franklin* was torturing prisoners. They still followed the old Geneva Convention codes of honour.

"I'll deal with it if it happens. Right now my focus is just on finding the Colonel and having a sit-down. I hear his wife is on board. That might work in our favour." Gill looked straight at him. Rico couldn't take his eyes off Gill.

He didn't care if he was giving himself away. Time was of the essence. They needed to end this meeting. But another question from someone at the table stopped him from stopping it.

"How so?"

"He'll be more aware and protective having his wife there," Gill assured him.

"You won't..." Manny paused before finishing the question.

Gill scoffed, "I'm not planning on hurting the woman. Of course, he doesn't need to know that." Gill winked. His blond hair still standing on end like he'd just got out of bed. Some of that from Rico's own hands. Gill's tats covered by his long-sleeved military shirt. The gauges in his ears looked out of place, but Rico wouldn't change a thing.

"Okay, that's all for now." Rico looked down at his watch. "We'll reconvene on the bridge at..." He stopped, wondering how much time he could give them before they started the mission. "Seventeen hundred hours. Dismissed."

Some of the others looked like they still had questions, but there really wasn't anything else to go over. It was pretty cut and dried.

Once everyone had left, Gill came to his side.

"Way to clear a room."

"I know, but I can't focus right now. I should be ashamed of myself, but I'm not. I want to use every second we have left. To live in this moment. We don't know what will happen after this, but, if we're both still alive, I want... God, Gill, I want to get to know you. I want this war over so we can... Fuck, I don't know...date?"

Gill threw back his head and laughed. "Date? I think we might be past that. Get to know each other, yes, but I'm thinking you need to move in with me."

"And how is that going to work, hotshot? I'm the Captain of a spaceship. You're the Captain of ground troops."

"We'll figure it out."

"What if you don't like me?"

"Won't happen."

"How can you be so sure?"

"I think fate had a hand in us meeting and I don't think she's finished with us just yet."

"I hope you're right, Gill. I really do." Rico pulled Gill in close and hugged him.

Just being in the moment, he closed his eyes and took a deep breath. He could stand here forever and never let him go.

"Let's go to your quarters."

Rico nodded and reluctantly released Gill. He took his hand and led him to his room. He had the real Gill here in front of him now and there were things he wanted to do.

The door closed behind them. Gill moved to go to the bed, but Rico stopped him.

"Not yet." He ran his fingers over Gill's face as if memorising him. He traced his lips and Gill licked the pad of his finger. Rico slipped the tip inside and pulled out. He refused to be distracted. Rico brushed his thumbs over Gill's eyebrows and kissed his eyelids closed. He ruffled Gill's hair and cupped his scalp, bringing their heads closer so he could brush his lips over Gill's lips, nipping the corners of his mouth. He wouldn't deepen the kiss no matter how Gill tried to get him to. He stroked Gill's back until he got to his ass and squeezed. He licked Gill's neck at the same time. Gill was salty and smelt heavenly. Rico ran his teeth over Gill's Adam's apple. He was going to explore every inch of the real Gill, leaving nothing to the imagination. When they were finished he would know Gill's body as well as his own. He wanted to know what turned Gill on.

Rico ran into Gill's shirt—it had to come off. He needed more skin. He took the bottom and raised it up and over Gill's head until that lean muscled chest was in front of him. Gill hadn't moved and kept his hands at his side until Rico took the shirt off. Once it was on the floor, Gill put his hands back to his side. Gill just moaned, his eyes closed and fingers twitching, as if he wanted to clutch at Rico. He was doing something right. Rico ran his teeth down to Gill's nipple and scraped over it. Gill went up on his tiptoes and hissed. Rico worried it with his teeth, pinching Gill's other nipple before soothing them with his tongue, one at a time. They were standing on end when Rico was done with them, so pretty and red. He continued his exploration of Gill's body.

He tongued his way down Gill's stomach, outlining his abs and wiggling his tongue into Gill's belly button. Gill snorted, but didn't stop him. He got to his knees and that was when he ran into Gill's pants. *Damn it.* He should have had him disrobe first, but then some of the fun would have been taken out of it. Rico unsnapped his pants and eased them over his hips. Gill wore no underwear, he hadn't noticed that earlier. If he had, the meeting would have been even hotter. Gill's cock popped out of the pants, hard and ready to go. Rico kissed the bead of pre-cum off the tip, sucking the head inside his mouth. Gill was salty with a hint of sweet. Rico could've sucked all day, but that was all Gill was getting. Rico had more body to explore. Soon, he'd have Gill's cock up his ass. Next time. This time he was going to make Gill come from his touch. He released Gill's cock. Gill rocked forward trying to get him to suck more.

Rico nuzzled into the juncture of Gill's thigh, breathing him in.

"Rico…it's so…big, please, please."

"Shh…" he soothed Gill.

Rico knew he wasn't talking about cocks. It was the feeling, very overwhelming, but oh so right.

"Don't know how much I can take." Gill reached for his cock, but Rico swatted his hand away.

"Mine. Stand still, Gill." He made his voice hard, using his command tone.

Gill's cock jerked, but his hands went back to his side and he clenched his fists.

"Please."

"Relax. Just…feel."

He unclenched his fists and wiggled his fingers. Satisfied that Gill would keep his position, Rico continued his journey. He bowed down and licked Gill's feet. Even his fuckin' toes were sexy. Who knew he'd have a foot fetish?

Gill whimpered above him. He looked up. Gill had never looked hotter. His eyes were hooded and he was panting, but still not moving. He thought of how subservient he looked bent down and kissing Gill's feet, but there was Gill, following Rico's demands.

"Turn around, Gill."

He whimpered, but obeyed. Rico could have crawled around him, but this was oh so much better. Having this strong brave man doing whatever Rico wanted. The power was great, but he wouldn't abuse it. He wanted to own every inch of the man in front of him.

Rico kissed Gill's heel and nibbled on his calf, tonguing his thighs and squeezing them before he got to that glorious ass. He'd been inside that, not too long ago. Rico wondered if he could still taste himself on Gill. It wasn't like they'd had a real good clean-up after the sex on the table. He bit the cheek before spreading Gill to see his pink pucker. He could have had Gill bend over, but this way was better, making him stand still while Rico played. He used his thumbs to stroke the pretty opening. He leaned in and nuzzled his face close, the smell of Gill intoxicating. Then he licked him and damn if he didn't taste of Rico. Gill rocked back and Rico let him have that bit. He was out of his mind with desire, fuck, he'd almost come from that taste alone and he had more body to explore. He reluctantly left Gill's ass and continued up his back, nipping at his tailbone before running his teeth and tongue along Gill's spine. He had to stand again to reach the back of Gill's neck and nuzzle into it. His hands stroking Gill's stomach as he rocked his body against Gill's, his cock nudging Gill's ass. He wanted inside again, but not yet.

"Fuuuckkkk... Rico... God, man you're killing me. Gotta... Please, more... Please, please, please."

"You want me inside you? How bad?" Rico squeezed Gill's cock and ran his finger over the tip, gathering up the pre-cum and licking it off.

"So bad. Please, please."

"No."

"Wha—"

"You're gonna fuck me, Gill."

"Rico..." Gill whined.

"You don't want that?" Rico whispered into Gill's ear, licking the lobe.

"Yes, but...fuck. So close, I'll come as soon as I touch your ass."

"You want to come now?"

"Yes, yes. Yes."

Rico stroked Gill's cock with one hand while using his other to put his cock between Gill's cheeks, rubbing himself off in time with each tug. They were going to come this way first and then Gill was going to fuck him once they recovered. They would spend the next few hours in a sex coma if necessary. He couldn't get enough of Gill and he never wanted to.

Gill went to his tiptoes. Rico caressed his balls, they were so tight and high, Gill was ready to come. For that matter, so was he.

"Come for me, Gill. Now."

Gill's ass clenched around his cock and just like that he came. The warmth of Gill's semen coated his hand. Rico brought it to his mouth and licked off Gill's cum. Gill turned and sucked on Rico's fingers, he dropped his hand and took Gill's mouth in a savage kiss. Gill wrapped a leg around Rico's hips and his arms around his body, circling him.

They broke away panting. Everything was so intense. Rico rested his forehead against Gill's. It was quickly becoming his favourite position.

They'd rest, but it was his turn next. He wanted to feel Gill's cock inside him.

Gill awoke from their short nap to find Rico curled around him. He kissed his shoulder and worked his way down Rico's body without waking him. Gill nudged him a little so Rico rolled onto his back. Just where he wanted him. Gill nuzzled his face into Rico's ass. The moan alerted him that his lover was awake. Gill spread his cheeks and licked from Rico's ass to his balls.

"Gill—" Rico moaned.

He couldn't say anything. Not right now, he wanted a taste of that ass. He circled the hole with his tongue before wiggling it inside. Rico tasted of sweet and something that was all him, a flavour Gill could quickly become addicted to.

Rico rocked back and Gill fucked his ass with his tongue. Licking and stroking as much as he could. But it wasn't enough. He wanted inside. Rico got up on his hands and knees.

"Fuck me, Gill."

Gill sucked on his middle finger before easing it inside.

"You're so tight."

"Just—now, Gill. Please."

"You're not ready. Let me—" He moved another finger inside and stretched the hole that his cock was going to be inside.

"Gill. Now!"

"Lube?" Gill removed his fingers and pressed his body to Rico's.

He licked and nuzzled Rico's neck before scraping his teeth along the column of Rico's throat giving him a little nibble.

Rico jerked away and moaned. He must have found a sensitive spot—he was going to have to try that again and often. He rubbed the spot with his thumb. Rico shuddered.

"No time—damn it, I want you inside me," Rico begged.

Gill spat in his hand and coated his cock.

"This is going to hurt."

"Don't care. I want the burn," Rico insisted.

Gill's cock kissed Rico's hole and he was about to push in when—

"Sir, you're being requested on the comms." The computer's tin voice echoed around the room.

This wasn't happening. Not now, not when he was so close to being a part of Rico.

"What the fuck?" Gill sat back on his heels, his cock so hard it hurt.

"Computer." Rico cleared his throat. "Computer, I'm not to be…" He gulped in some air. "Disturbed."

Gill had no idea how he made a coherent sentence. He could barely think of one, much less speak. He was seconds away from being inside Rico for the first time, damn it. He should have listened and taken Rico when he'd demanded it.

Note to self, always listen to Rico.

He would have laughed if he hadn't been in so much pain.

"Yes, sir, but this is coded as an emergency."

"Give me a second and I'll be right there."

Rico collapsed onto the bed.

"Rico—" He knew it sounded like a whine, but he couldn't help himself.

"Fuck. I know. This better be good or heads will roll." Rico got off the bed and started to dress.

Gill did laugh as Rico struggled to stuff his hard dick into his pants, cursing the whole time.

"Laugh it up, but you'd better get dressed too. If this is an emergency we'll both be needed."

"Aw, shit!"

Now Rico laughed. Maybe later the whole situation would be funny, but at that moment, as he was dressing, Gill was grumpy. He scrambled off the bed and put on his shirt. He had no idea where his pants were.

"We'll get back to this." Rico grabbed him by his shirt and gave him a hard kiss.

He could deal with later as long as there was one. He would have Rico's ass.

Chapter Eight

"They're out there."

"Sir?"

Scott shook off the sense of foreboding.

"The Alliance has a ship out there."

"Should we get to battle stations?"

"Not yet. Let me think." Scott was so tired. Too tired. He'd let this go on far too long and he'd lost valuable members of his staff. He could be wrong about the ship, but he didn't think so. Should he just surrender and get this over with? The year had been hard. They weren't losing, but they weren't winning either and people were dying. People that he'd sworn to protect. If it went on too much longer, he would lose, but it wouldn't only be him. He'd seen pictures of what his actions had cost the Earth. It was barren and dying and it was all his fault. But he was doing the right thing, wasn't he?

America shouldn't be governed by a coalition.

"Why not?" His wife had sneaked up behind him and wrapped her arms around him. He hadn't realised he'd said it out loud.

"That's not what America is about. It has rules and—the Constitution and the proper chain of command with the President in the lead."

"So?"

"What do you mean, so?"

"Who rules the galaxy?"

"No one really." Scott shrugged and wondered where she was going with this.

"So who was it you talked to when we took over Alto and made it our own?"

"The Consortium."

"And how did that work out for us?"

"Okay. Well…good, but what's your point?"

"My point is, it works. We should join them and show them Alto. That should have been our mission from the beginning and I think deep down inside you know it."

Scott sighed. "What about this whole year? I can't forget and neither can they. We've all but destroyed the planet."

"I know they can't, but hail them anyway. Welcome that ship aboard and let's get on with our lives. End it now while we still can. If we do, maybe they'll accept our help because you know they're going to need it."

"Nancy—"

"I'm pregnant, Scott, and I want to go home."

He turned around. "What?"

He couldn't have heard her right.

"Yes, we're having a baby. Now stop this stupid war and take me home."

"But…we don't know what kind of harm could come to the baby when we warp to the planet."

"That's a chance we have to take. I'm not having your son or daughter here in space during a war. Now fix it!" She slapped his chest and left.

Scott rubbed a hand over the sore spot. His wife packed a punch, in more ways than one. He was going to be a daddy. Fuck. He slumped down and fell to the floor, his head in his hands. He should have never listened to his Earth-bound contact. He knew that now, but he'd panicked and now look what he'd done. The wrong thing. And he *was* the villain of this piece. He should have contacted the Alliance from the start and not shown force. Things might have gone a different way. He needed to find out why his contact, Alice, had gone to all this trouble to help him start the war. But that was for another day. Right now he had people to welcome aboard. It was time to end this.

He stood up and headed for the bridge.

"Lieutenant, hail any Alliance ship in the vicinity."

"Sir?"

"Do it," Scott commanded.

"Yes, sir."

It took a few minutes, but they were on the line, vocal only.

"This is Captain Ricardo Clark of the *Annihilation*."

"Captain Clark, this is Colonel Scott Winchester and I think we need to have a face-to-face talk. I'd like to offer my ship up for the meeting."

"I'm not sure I understand, Colonel." The disbelief came through loud and clear.

Scott took a deep breath and just let it all out. "It's time to end this, don't you think?"

There was a stunned silence. He would have been the same way if he'd been on the other end. It was out of the blue and he was sure the Alliance didn't expect him to be the one encouraging a ceasefire. After all, he *had* been the one to start this mess.

"I'm not sure if that is a good idea, Colonel. What reassurances do I have that you won't take me or members of my crew as prisoners?"

"I'll make it more social. My wife will be in attendance. I'll need *your* assurance that there will be no weapons brought on board."

He didn't know how smart that was, but he knew she'd want to be there and she had earned that right. He would have to trust the Alliance to follow treaty protocol.

"I'm sorry, Colonel, but I'll need to have at least one armed guard while going onto an enemy vessel."

"I'll concede to one guard."

It was the least he could agree to. If it were him, he would have demanded at least five armed men.

"We aren't that far out, we'll be there in half an hour."

"We'll be waiting."

He ended the communication.

"Lieutenant, I need you to get all of our ships on the line. We have a half hour to make some plans."

The conference call didn't take long and he had some relieved men and women on his hands. They were just as tired as he was and wanted to go home. Scott was stubborn, but not pigheaded. He knew when it was time to quit and Alto had become his home. He was ready to see his house and sleep in his own bed for a change.

Scott went to find his wife.

"Nancy, I need you to come to the war room with me. I've invited members of the Alliance to meet here and I told them you'd be there."

He stood in the doorway. His wife really was beautiful with her long black hair and deep blue eyes. It was hard to believe he was going to be a daddy. He hoped that it would look like her and would have her temperament. They needed more people with a calming influence in the family. Maybe a little girl, the spitting image of her mother. They had about seven months, maybe less, to get things under control. They could do it.

"Good. This is really good. I'm thankful you listened to me." She glided over to him.

"Me too, sweetheart. I should have listened to you from the beginning, but Alice made things seem so bad down there."

"Well, you *know* what I think of Alice."

"I know, I know. But, Nancy, you have to agree, the things she said…"

"You'll have to let these Alliance people know. Our stopping this might not be the end of the war with them if Alice is still stirring things up."

Scott pulled her in and kissed the top of her head.

"How much time do we have?" She nuzzled into his shoulder.

"They should be here in a few minutes. I wanted to change into my formal uniform."

"Why did you take so long to tell me!" She pushed away and raced around the room.

"I had to let the others know what was happening."

They both dressed in record time and headed to the war room. He was happy for the first time since the war had begun. The world shouldn't be torn in two like it had been. Scott should have taken his cues and ended this when other nations had joined in with the Alliance, but he'd let old friendships colour his vision. The blinders had dropped and it was time to do the right thing.

They'd reached the room and seconds later the comms sounded.

"Sir, the visitors are here. Their ship just boarded."

His wife went to the refreshment area to get it ready, mumbling about wishing she had more time, and he went to sit at the head of the table.

"How many?" Scott tapped a finger on the arm of his chair.

"Two men."

That wasn't bad, not a show of force at all. He could handle two men. For that matter so could his wife. She might not be enlisted, but she swung a mean right hook and knew her way around a weapon. Thinking of guns…

"Were they scanned for weapons?"

"Yes, there is one laser between the two of them."

He was relieved. The whole meeting could end in disaster and he really didn't want it to start off on the wrong foot.

"Good, show them in."

Chapter Nine

"I'm not sure this is the greatest idea," Gill whispered to Rico.

He didn't have a bad feeling per se, but they were supposed to be covert about this, not walk onto the enemy's ship at their invitation. He'd been arguing about it from the beginning. Of course, he wasn't happy because they'd been hailed right before he was going to sink his cock balls-deep into Rico for the first time, damn it. But that wasn't the only reason. This Colonel could have ulterior motives. And only letting them bring one gun?

Gill had wanted to bring more men too, but Rico had said the Colonel's wife would be there and he didn't want a show of force. He was just happy Rico had chosen him to go along with him. He could have left Gill's troops on board and taken his second-in-command.

"We could end the war right here and right now. It's worth the risk. We both have seconds-in-command on the *Annihilation* who will fire on this ship if we're harmed. I don't think he'd invite his wife to a meeting with the enemy if he was planning something."

So that was why he'd picked Gill for the ride-along. But not planning something because a woman would be there? That was just going in blind. Women could be just as deadly as men. As a matter of fact he had a group of them in his troops. Bloodthirsty, the lot of them.

"You don't know that."

"No, I don't, but we both have the training to get out of this if we need to."

"We only have one weapon."

"Weapons are for sissies." Rico winked at him.

Gill just grinned. How could Rico be so relaxed?

They docked the skimmer and were met by a woman in uniform. She told them to follow her and they were escorted to another room. It was almost like he was walking back onto the *Annihilation*. Maybe all warships looked the same. The crew on the *Franklin* looked as worn down as his own. The war had taken its toll on all of them. Gill let loose some of the tension he'd been carrying. They weren't there with guns blazing and weren't treating him and Rico like they were criminals. Maybe things would be okay.

The door opened to a handsome couple. The man, Colonel Winchester he assumed, was sitting down and his wife was standing behind him with her hand on his shoulder. She had long black hair that draped down her back and blue eyes that seemed to smile. Her husband looked grimmer with short brown hair and brown eyes that were cold. Gill's heart paused for a beat before speeding up. This man was a killer and here he was with his lover and only one weapon between the two of them. How was he going to protect Rico?

The Colonel stood and his wife moved to his side.

"Hello, I'm Colonel Scott Winchester and this is my wife, Nancy Winchester."

Rico moved closer and Gill tensed. He was being silly. Rico could take care of himself.

"I'm Captain Ricardo Clark and this is my partner, Captain Gilliland Carter."

Gill did a double-take before holding out his hand. Colonel Winchester's handshake was as hard as he was. His wife had a gentler touch.

"So you two..." The Colonel didn't finish his sentence.

Rico stepped back and rested his hand on Gill's lower back. He didn't unclench, though. He would stay tight and on point until he felt more comfortable. He wouldn't let his guard down.

"Yes, Colonel, Gill is my partner in every way." Rico nodded his head.

"Please call him Scott and I'm Nancy. Let's sit down and get started. Please." Nancy smiled.

Gill liked her. "Then I'm Gill and he's Rico." He walked around the table and put the window to his back so he had a clear line of sight to the door. He didn't want to be sneaked up on. Rico followed his lead.

He hadn't expected Rico to tell this couple about them, but he did see it relaxed Scott. It was just two couples having a nice chat. How smart was Rico? He should have known there was more behind him being there than just as a gun hand.

"You called this meeting. What is it you want?" Rico folded his hands on the table and looked at Scott.

"I'm ready for this to end. I made a grievous error and I'd like to rectify it."

"This won't bring back all the dead. Why should we stop now?" Rico was calm and didn't flinch. He would need to ask the hard questions so he could report back to the Commandant.

"No. It won't. It might have taken me a while, but I've found out that I am here under false pretences. I was led to believe that things were different down on Earth."

"You do know that the Earth will not be able to sustain life in just a few short years, don't you? And you know why?"

Scott hung his head down low and his wife stroked his shoulders. Gill reached under the table and squeezed Rico's leg. Rico took his hand in his.

"It's my fault and they're my weapons. I am very aware. If I could change the last year, I would, but I can't. The only thing I can do now is make amends and help clear the planet, but I think I'm the least of your worries right now."

Gill couldn't believe the man. It had taken him a year to figure out that the war was pointless? All the lives that had been lost and the destruction of an entire planet and he was just saying — oopsy, my bad? Not to mention all the time Gill could have been getting to know Rico. What a waste. It pissed him off and he wanted to say 'fuck it' and shoot the guy then and there, but he didn't think Rico would like that. Good thing he was the one doing the talking or this could go a very different way. Rico seemed to have a cooler head. Thank goodness one of them did.

"Why is that?"

He couldn't believe how calm Rico sounded.

Yep, the right man is in charge.

"My contact on Earth, Alice Cole, told me horror stories of the Alliance and how they had overthrown the government and taken over. I believed her. I didn't have a reason not to. She sent me an S.O.S. that finally arrived and I acted hastily. I've talked to the other ships and we've agreed to join the Alliance and start preparation for evacuation."

"I'll have to get in touch with the Commandant and the two of you will have to meet to make this formal, but I don't see a problem with that. And I recognise that name. Why?" Rico turned to look at Gill.

Well, that made a bit more sense, but, still, he'd never get those moments back. And that name... He'd heard it before.

"I'm not sure — it does sound vaguely... Wait — isn't that the woman who wanted to become the next President and said she fell next in the line of succession?"

"That's her. So she started this because she wasn't in power?" Rico looked at Scott again.

"Why am I not surprised?" Nancy sighed. "All of this could have been prevented. Someone needs to stop Alice or she'll try something else."

"We should schedule a meeting soon. Once Alice finds out we're backing off, who knows what she'll try. I didn't realise how power-hungry she'd become. I'm ashamed of myself." Scott let out a sigh.

Gill could feel a bit sorry for the guy. He was trying to be loyal and he'd fucked up. Gill could tell he felt awful about the situation by the slump in his shoulders. The proud man they'd seen when they'd walked into the room was gone and in his place was the picture of defeat. Gill wasn't as pissed off as he'd been earlier. He couldn't worry about the past right now — it was time to think towards the future and maybe get back to a time when it was peaceful.

"She was a friend and you were doing your job." Rico let Scott off the hook. "We'll set up a meeting and get back to you."

"So, why were you out there?" Scott asked.

Gill had wondered when Scott would ask about that. Scott wasn't a stupid man and the *Annihilation* had been really close to his position. Closer than any other ship had been in months.

"Excuse me?" Rico cocked his head.

Gill liked how Rico played it. Making Scott ask straight out what he wanted.

"You were only thirty minutes away from my ship. Why?" Scott asked again.

Rico had to answer this time and Gill waited to hear what he'd say.

"Fair enough. We were here to force a talk with you to quit this destruction. You weren't listening to the Alliance and we had to do something."

"By force?" Scott questioned.

He didn't sound angry, only curious.

"Well, we weren't going to fire on you unless you shot first and Gill here was going to breach your ship and get to you. To talk." Rico stressed that last part.

That was why he was in charge and not Gill. He knew the right words without making a bad situation worse. He'd been right all along, Rico was meant to be in charge.

"Ah, I see. How was he going to manage that?" Scott looked at him.

"That's classified." Gill winked at Scott. "Maybe after you join the Alliance I'll be able to tell you. We should get back to the ship so we can put our call in. The sooner we can start evacuation the better."

If Rico could take the high ground so could Gill.

"I agree. I'm going to try and contact Alice. If I find her location, I'll comms you. We need to stop this and not exacerbate the situation."

"Will you be heading back to Earth right away or staying here in orbit?" Nancy asked as they stood.

"My guess is the Commandant will want us to stay here and work on negotiations."

"Good, then you'll have to come back for supper. We'll see you tonight." Nancy left the room.

Rico stood with his mouth open. Gill reached over and shut it for him.

"My wife is a force of nature." Scott laughed.

"I like her." Gill smiled back.

"I guess we'll see you tonight." Rico nodded and left the room.

"Scott, here is the information I was supposed to talk with you about. Maybe you should take a look while you're trying to find Alice."

Gill left the tablet with the information on the flood and what had happened to the President and why the Alliance had stepped in, then raced to follow Rico.

"Well, that went better than expected." Gill squeezed Rico's arm.

"Was it too easy?" Rico looked worried.

"I don't think so. Why?" They'd reached the skimmer and got inside, Gill behind the wheel.

"It's just... We have been at this for a year with no break from the Old Guard and now, out of the blue, we have a truce and they're going to join the Alliance. To top it off, they're going to help us get people off of Earth." Rico strapped himself in.

"I think Scott's wife might have had something to do with it. I knew who's in charge in *that* family. And I left him the data on the flood so he could read up on what really happened." Gill flipped a couple of switches and they disembarked the *Franklin*.

"You could be right. I just don't want to get my hopes up. Hopefully the intel will help the situation."

"Let me distract you. Call the Commandant and meet me in your room."

Chapter Ten

Rico was distracted. The meeting *had* gone well and he felt really good about that, but his mind was on Gill back in his room.

"Manny, patch me through to the Commandant."

"Yes, sir. Good news?"

"Very."

Moments later a voice come over the computer system.

"This is Commandant Walker."

"Sir, this is Captain Ricardo Clark, reporting as ordered."

"Tell me you have good news, son. Was Captain Carter able to breach the ship?"

"He didn't have to, sir. They invited us on board."

"What? Did I hear that right?"

"You did, sir. Colonel Winchester reached out to us in a ceasefire. He was given faulty information from one Alice Cole. He was told the Alliance overthrew the President and was a tyrannical organisation. Once we sat down and spoke, he admitted the error of his ways and said he'd like to join the Alliance as well as help us get folks off Earth and settled elsewhere. He'd like a meeting with you. Captain Carter and myself will be eating dinner with him and his wife tonight." Rico had no idea why he added the last part, but it felt like the right thing to do.

"Good job, Captain. I know about that troublemaker, Ms Cole. She's been causing a stir for a few years now. We didn't know she'd carried it this far."

"The Colonel is getting her whereabouts right now and will comms me when he has them. As soon as I know, you'll know."

"Very nice. You're going places, young man. I'll put you in for a promotion. Before you know it, you'll be after my job." The Commandant chuckled.

Rico shuddered at the thought of running an organisation like the Alliance. It would never happen. The comms went dark before he could respond.

"That is good news, sir. About the promotion *and* the Old Guard coming around."

"I really can't take credit."

It had been all Scott. He'd only shown up. Sure, things could have gone differently if Gill had infiltrated Scott's ship, but it hadn't happened that way so he couldn't take the praise for the surrender.

"Doesn't matter, you're getting it." Manny laughed.

Rico shook his head. "I'm going to my quarters. Don't disturb me unless there is an emergency. I mean it this time. Unless we're being blown out of the sky, take care of it."

"Yes, sir." Manny winked at him.

Rico left the command centre shaking his head and followed the corridor to his room. He didn't expect to find a naked Gill, but he shouldn't have been surprised.

"All done?"

"Ah, yeah." He took off his clothes and set them aside, joining Gill.

"And what did the Commandant have to say?" Gill kissed his neck.

God, that was a hot spot for him and, ever since Gill had found out, he'd attacked it at will.

"I get a promotion," Rico managed to say.

It was hard with all the outside stimuli. In a short time, Gill had him figured out.

"That's good," Gill murmured against his throat.

"Yep. Um...do you really want to talk about this right now?" Rico squirmed.

"No." Gill sank his teeth into Rico's shoulder and then licked away the burn.

"Okay then. We only have a few hours until dinner."

"Whatever shall we do?" Gill smirked.

"I think we were interrupted earlier. Something to do with your cock in my ass."

"I do seem to recall that."

"Good, let me get the rope."

"Huh...what?" Gill looked confused.

"Oh, you thought you'd be in charge? Nope. I'm tying you to the bed and having my way with you."

"But—"

"Don't worry, your cock will still be so far inside me we won't know who is who. I'll be riding you, babe."

Rico gave Gill a wicked grin.

"I...you...ah..."

Rico pushed Gill on the bed.

"Yes, you and me. Now stay there, I'm going to get some ties." Rico turned and searched through his drawers. He had to have something he could use.

There they were. His mother had insisted that he bring some of his ties. He had no idea why and now he didn't care, but he would be thanking her. He pulled them out of the drawer along with the lube and turned. Gill was sprawled out on the bed and had his hands wrapped around the headboard. It was fuckin' hot as all get-out.

"Damn, you're spectacular, Gill." Rico crawled onto the bed and brushed his body over Gill's and sucked on his lower lip.

Gill moved his hands and Rico let him get away with it for a second.

"No touching."

The whimper made him smile. This was going to be fun.

"Rico..."

"I'm going to use you now, Gill. You ready?"

"Fuck."

"I'll take that as a yes."

He bent Gill's arms at the elbow and tied his wrists to the headboard.

"Is that too tight, Gill? Are you comfortable?"

"I..." Gill was panting.

"Calm down or I'll stop. Take a deep breath. That's it, let it go. Again. Now, is that too tight?"

Gill shook his head.

"Okay. Good." Rico slid his hand down Gill's chest, resting it so he could feel the heartbeat. It was still erratic, but Gill was controlling his breathing now. It was time.

He turned around, straddled Gill and put his ass in his face.

"Rico. Please."

Rico didn't answer. He opened the lube and put some on his fingers and leant forward more, balancing on one arm while he reached around and played with his ass. He eased a finger in, then another until he was rocking back and forth, teasing Gill. Rico moved forward just a bit to take Gill's cock into his mouth. He moaned around the long, thick thing of beauty.

"Rico, Rico—"

Gill was vibrating, but not thrusting into his mouth. Rico could feel Gill holding back. Not waiting for Gill to come, he eased off, lightly running his teeth along Gill's length, and took his fingers out of his ass at the same time.

He picked the lube back up from where he'd thrown it and coated Gill's cock before turning around. He looked into Gill's eyes as he eased himself down inch by slow agonising inch. He wanted to slam himself onto Gill, but he had a bit more control than that.

Rico hissed as Gill's thick cock stretched his body.

Gill was straining against the binding, the veins in his neck standing out as he tried not to thrust. Rico rewarded him for his restraint by moving up and then slamming his body down. Gill was all the way inside him.

"So full, Gill."

"Move. Damn it. Move," Gill said through clenched teeth.

For that, Rico stopped all movement. Gill twitched under him, but didn't thrust. He did clutch at the ties on his hands. Rico tightened his ass and milked Gill's cock, still not moving.

"Please, please, please."

That was what he was waiting for and he was happy Gill had said it because he was losing control fast. He bent over and untied one of Gill's hands.

"Jack me off." He kissed Gill's wrist and wrapped his fingers around his dick.

He groaned, but bounced up and down on Gill's cock. He was so close and the sensation from Gill's hand was almost too much, but not enough. He reached over and undid the other tie, moving so he could help Gill sit up. Gill released Rico's dick and wrapped his arms around Rico. Rico did the same and they were wrapped around each other. Gill thrust up, meeting each of Rico's movements. His cock was trapped between their bodies and rubbing against Gill's stomach.

Rico buried his face into Gill's shoulder, his movement becoming frantic.

"Rico…now, now, now." Gill dug his feet into the bed and thrust up as Rico slammed down, his cum splashing between them and Gill's hot release seeping from his ass.

"Fuck, fuck, fuck. Gill." He was kissing any skin he could get to and Gill smoothed a hand down his back.

Rico still moved his hips. He couldn't stop until Gill finally softened enough to slide out of him. Rico shivered.

They came down from the rush and Rico slid off Gill, bringing them both to lie down on the bed. He didn't release his hold. He couldn't if he wanted to. He never wanted to let Gill go again and he didn't care if things were happening too fast. He'd only live once and he was going to take these feelings and run with them. He didn't care what he had to do to make it happen.

"We should shower," Gill muttered.

"Soon. I just want to hold you."

"M'kay."

He closed his eyes and he could see the two of them like this for a very long time. He just hoped that Gill felt the same way.

Chapter Eleven

Gill couldn't stop smiling. It seemed to be his day. His ass might be sore and he was sure Rico's was too, but that wouldn't make the smile go away. He was with the guy he'd had fantasies about for a long time and it looked like he wasn't the only one who was happy. Rico winked at him as they boarded the craft that would take them back to the *Franklin*.

"I'm hungry." Gill rubbed his stomach.

"We have had a workout today." Rico smacked his ass.

"Hey!" He sat down and had to shift around to get comfortable.

Rico gave him a knowing look and he had to chuckle. *Aren't we a pair?*

It didn't take long and the two of them enjoyed the comfortable silence between them. It was nice to not feel like he had to fill the space with nonsense.

"Welcome back. The Colonel would like you to join him in his quarters." The same twink from earlier led them down a long corridor and stopped at a double door. It slid open into a big room. A table had been set up and it looked like it would be just the four of them present.

"Good evening. I hope you're hungry. Nancy put together a feast."

"I could eat." Rico winked at him.

"Good, good. Have a seat." Scott waved them to the table.

"Thanks." Gill sat down. "It smells great."

"It's good as it can be from a computer. When we get back to Alto and you guys get settled, well… If you end up there, you'll have to come by and I'll cook you a real meal."

"I'd like that. So, tell us a little about this planet."

"Well most of it was uninhabited when we found it. It's a lot like Earth, not too many differences. We landed and started to explore when we were approached by the solar systems' governing body. We put in a request to stay and explore. They didn't have a problem with it. We started building houses. Our ship wasn't the only one to find other planets. Some of them thriving. There is a lot of uncharted space out there and most of it empty. At least from what we've found."

"Were they all human?"

"For the most part, yes, they appeared as we do. But more advanced. They helped us out with translators so we could understand anyone who happened to stop by," Scott answered.

"So you have a contact the Alliance can go to? Will we all fit on Alto?" Rico dug into his meal as he talked.

Gill just listened. He was a grunt and not big on the political aspects of ruling. It looked like Rico was, though. He wondered at that. Rico was very smart. Before he knew it, his lover would probably be running the place. Wouldn't that be odd, but it seemed fitting. He had a big presence about him and people tended to listen.

The ship shook.

"What the hell was that?" Gill looked around and held onto the table.

It happened again. Something was very wrong.

"Shields activated. Code Red. Code Red. Enemy fire detected." The computer repeated the same thing every couple of minutes.

"Nancy, stay here. Lock yourself in. I don't suppose the two of you can explain this?" Scott looked pissed off.

"Like we would sit down to dinner with you and have our ship fire. Please, give us credit for not being stupid. This isn't from us and it isn't from the Alliance. We conferred with the Commandant. He's happy for a sit-down."

"Come with me." Scott strode out of the door.

Gill followed Scott and Rico. They made it quickly to the bridge.

"Report," Scott demanded.

"A large craft appeared in our space and fired two missiles. We were able to raise our shields, but there is some damage to the cargo bay. Colonel, we're being hailed."

"Open up the line, voice and video activated," Scott demanded.

Gill's heart was racing. This was unexpected. They'd called a truce. Why was someone firing on the *Franklin*? Was the *Annihilation* okay? He looked over at Rico who looked just as worried as Gill felt.

"Yes, sir." The man at the helm pushed a few buttons.

A woman's face appeared on the screen. Gill didn't recognise her, but he did know that ship. It was one of the Alliance's.

"Alice, what the fuck are you doing?"

Wasn't that the woman Scott had told them about? The one who'd caused this whole thing to begin with?

"What I should have done all along. I'm taking control."

Gill expected a mad laugh to follow, but the woman's eyes were cold. She was crazy. There was no other explanation.

"You and what army?" Scott crossed his arms over his chest and glared.

"I have my resources." She grinned and cut communications. Another blast rocked the ship.

"Colonel, I'm showing a breach on this deck." The helmsman looked back to where Scott stood and worried his lip, like he didn't want to tell Scott bad news.

"Where?" Scott demanded.

Gill didn't have a good feeling about this. It was off. Something in the woman's expression bothered him, but he couldn't put his finger on it.

"Your quarters."

Gill didn't wait for Scott to run out, he made a mad dash in the direction they'd come from earlier. The room was a wreck and Nancy was nowhere to be seen.

"Computer, locate Nancy." Scott appeared calm, but Gill knew it was a facade.

"She is not on the ship, sir."

"God damn it." Scott slammed his fist against the door.

He pushed a button on the wall. "Track that ship. Don't you fucking lose it. Alice has Nancy."

"We need to contact the Alliance." Rico was ever the calm voice of reason.

"Why would they help me?" Scott ran a hand through his hair and paced back and forth.

"You're a part of them now." Gill assured him.

"Not officially."

"Doesn't matter. They want this crap to end as much as you do. This will be a good-faith gesture. I need to let my second know as well so we can get the *Annihilation* on the trail too. She was on an Alliance craft. We might be able to track her that way." Rico headed back to the bridge.

"Where would she go and why would she take your wife? Something doesn't add up here, Scott." Gill hung back so he could get some information from Scott, his detective skills coming in handy.

Scott sighed. "Alice and I are friends from way back. Our families knew each other. There was never anything between us. She might have wanted it, but I never did. She was rude to Nancy a lot. I think she was jealous, but this is outside the realm of normal. Who does this?"

"She's power-hungry, Scott, and she thought she had you where she wanted you. Maybe she found out about the deal with the Alliance."

"But how?"

"You heard her, she has her sources. My guess would be a spy on the ship or someone in the Commandant's office."

"If it's someone here, we'll find them. Maybe they know where she's going." Scott seemed satisfied with that.

When they got to the bridge, Rico had taken over. It was the wrong time, but Gill got hard. There was something about Rico's commanding ways that made him hot. He couldn't help it.

"Captain Clark has full rein, give him what he wants. I'm going to start talking to each and every one of you in the war room. Alice Cole took Nancy and if someone here helped they'd better tell me because, if something happens to my wife, there will be holy hell to pay. Do I make myself clear?"

A timid voice spoke up. "I...it was...me. I'm *so* sorry. She didn't say she was going to do this. I was just supposed to let her know what was going on. I didn't think it was a bad thing... I mean...we're here because of her. Right? Oh my God, Colonel, I am so sorry."

Scott took his crewman by the shirt and held him up to his face.

"Where the fuck would she take her?" Scott's voice was deathly quiet.

Gill moved closer so Scott didn't kill the man.

"I have...here..." He reached behind him for a pad and shoved it at Scott. Scott dropped him.

Scott's hands were shaking. Gill looked over and Rico was still at the comms. He took the pad from Scott and read the coordinates. He looked at the man on the floor.

"Punch this in now and get us there," Gill demanded. The guy scrambled to follow his orders.

Gill got Scott to sit down in the captain's chair and went to Rico.

"We have a lead, here are the coordinates. You should have *Annihilation* meet us there. Let my crew know to be prepared for a fight."

Chapter Twelve

Rico couldn't believe it. They'd finally called a truce and now this shit. He'd better not get his hands on this Alice first or he'd throttle her himself. And he liked Nancy. She'd better be unharmed. He'd learned from Scott that Nancy was pregnant. This ordeal couldn't be good for her.

And he wasn't on his own ship. He shouldn't have taken over like he did, but Scott was a basket case. Not that he blamed him. He'd be the same way if something happened to Gill. Hard as it was to believe, but Gill had wormed his way into his heart in a quick amount of time. Once this was over, they were taking a vacation, damn it.

"We're here, Captain Clark."

"Good, lock her into orbit and we'll take a shuttle about five klicks away from the house. I want to give us a good space to fight if we have to. Relay that order to the Alliance and have my first mate meet us in the docking bay as well as Captain Carter's second-in-command. We'll convene at the cargo bay doors and take the shuttle from there. The Alliance has been notified and the Commandant might patch through. If he does, contact me right away."

"Yes, sir."

The ship's crew had no issue with taking his orders. That made things easier.

"Scott, are you staying here?" Rico clasped Scott's shoulder.

"Fuck no. I'm ready." Scott stood up.

Gill was at his side, his laser at the ready. "Let's do this."

"We need to go in slow. This is her home turf and she has the advantage. We don't know where Nancy is so be careful."

"Got it."

They reached the cargo bay and Manny was there as well as Slone, Gill's second-in-command.

"All right, people. Let's go in guns hot, but stay low and on the lookout. There is a civilian being held hostage. I want a quick in and out. Understood?"

"Yes, sir," the group replied in unison.

"Good, I'll take point. Scott, bring up the rear. Gill, you're middle man. Everyone else fall in. Slow and steady. Don't shoot unless you are fired upon and, like I said, watch out for the civilian. Once I ID Alison Cole, you can shoot to kill."

Rico was done with this. Alice had started this shit and he was going to finish it so things could get back to normal.

Everyone nodded and loaded into the shuttle. It didn't take long to reach the ground. They crept their way down a path. It wasn't wide so they really did have to go one after the other. Rico kept an ear cocked, listening for anything out of sync. And there it was. A scream. He held up a hand. Behind him, he could sense Scott's desperation to bolt in, but that could make things worse. He looked back at Gill and nodded towards Scott. They didn't even have to say a word. Gill dropped back and tapped his second on the back, pointing to Rico. Slone moved up beside Rico.

"Ready?" Rico whispered.

Slone gave a short nod. They crouched down and belly-crawled to the house. There was a lot of foliage so they were able to keep low and out of the way. There was a window open and they could hear talking. Not that Rico could make out the words — he was too focused on not being caught.

He couldn't think of Scott or even Gill. Right now it was all about Nancy.

The click of a weapon stopped him in his tracks.

"If you don't want the rest of your crew to die, you'll keep moving my way. We're going on a little trip and you just provided me better leverage. Thank you, Captain Clark."

Rico raised his head just enough to see who had spoken to him. It was Alice. When had he got so slow? This shouldn't have been possible, but now he was being taken prisoner and if he wanted to keep Gill alive he wouldn't give anything away. He had to make sure that he was the only one taken. He didn't want Alice to get her hands on more people. Rico did the only thing he could think of, he kicked back, smacking Slone in the head, knocking him unconscious and making him dead weight. She wouldn't want to haul Slone along, hopefully. He dragged Slone up near him and hoped the others couldn't see what he was doing. Rico took his comms unit tracker and put it down his own pants, making his movement small so she couldn't see what he was doing, leaving the other bit with Slone. He hoped Gill would get the clue. No way was he getting lost with this crazy woman.

"Just me," he whispered and kept moving forward until he reached the outer wall.

Alice dragged him forward and he didn't resist. Her ship stood behind the place. The only good thing about the location of her hideout was the launching pads for the spacecrafts. In seconds the group would know something was off, but he couldn't think about that now. He had to stay alive. People were counting on him.

"You can leave Nancy here, you know."

Alice backhanded him. "Shut up."

Rico clenched his teeth. He wanted to cold-cock the bitch, but now wasn't the right time. He couldn't see Nancy. He was pushed up the walkway and he stumbled a bit. Once he'd cleared the doorway the ship vibrated and did a vertical jump. Rico fell forward and dropped to the floor from the force of gravity. He wasn't expecting her to leave without letting him strap in. It was a little shuttle, not much room at all in the cockpit area. There was a door so there must've been another room or two back there. Alice had taken a seat by the pilot and didn't look back at him. Rico moved, but it didn't help. He was slammed to the ground again, hitting his head on something. His vision become fuzzy and he hit his head again. Darkness closed in.

* * * *

When he woke up, Rico was tied to a chair. His head fucking hurt like a son of bitch and he was a little foggy as to what had happened.

"Rico, are you okay?"

He knew that voice… It was… Rico closed his eyes and tried to concentrate. Nancy! Yes, it was Scott's wife and he was supposed to rescue her.

"Yeah, Nancy. Head hurts. You okay?" He turned to the sound of her voice. She was also tied up.

"She hasn't hurt me, yet. I was worried about you. You've been out for a while. They dragged you in here and you've been so still."

"I hit my head on liftoff." He closed his eyes again against the throb, but it wasn't helping him.

"Guess I was lucky to be locked down in here." Nancy sighed.

"Do you know where we're going?" He cracked open an eye and peered at her.

"Alice has been bragging. We're headed to Alto. She said that if she couldn't have Earth she'd have the next best thing."

"Not gonna happen. And we're on an Alliance ship, they don't have warp capabilities. How is she going to get there?"

"And how do you propose we stop it? I have no idea, but she seems pretty confident."

"Well, she's crazy and Gill will be here soon."

"How can you be so sure?"

"I left him a clue. He should be able to…" He paused. No way could he say anything more. Alice could be listening and he was being a chatty Cathy. No more of that.

"Rico?" She sounded worried.

"Sorry, just a feeling. Has she been back in since I was dropped off?" Rico looked around the room trying to see if there was a way he could escape. Maybe they could take over the ship. But he didn't know how many people were on board and he needed his head to stop pounding.

"No. They've left us alone."

"Good, that's good. Do you know how many people are on board?"

"I saw at least three, but she pushed me in here pretty fast. I don't have a clear head count."

"Fuck. All right, can you get untied?"

"I've been trying, but so far no luck."

"So how long was I out?"

"I would say a couple of hours, but I'm not completely sure. We don't have a clock and time can be tricky when you're a captive."

She was right. A minute could seem like a half an hour. He had to prepare for the worst. It wasn't going to get better anytime soon.

Chapter Thirteen

"What the fuck just happened?" Gill looked in disbelief as the spacecraft launched out of the atmosphere.

"Fuck!" Scott broke away and charged into the clearing.

Gill followed. Slone lay on the ground and he was out cold. This wasn't good. Gill crouched down and turned Slone over. A comms unit fell off him. Gill picked it up and looked it over. It had to be Rico's and the tracking chip was activated, a light blinked back at him.

"Yes."

"Why are you *happy*? Rico and Nancy are gone." Scott turned on him.

"They are, but"—Gill kissed the comm—"Rico left us a way to get them back. We need to get to the *Annihilation*. We're going to take that bitch down and smile while we're doing it." Gill laughed.

"What. The. Fuck?" Scott looked confused.

Gill really hadn't explained it well.

"Rico has a tracking unit on him or on the ship he's on. We need the *Annihilation* to put in the codes and get the hustle on." He bent over and put Slone over his shoulder and ran back to the others. "We need to get back to the *Annihilation*. Captain Clark has been taken hostage along with Mrs Winchester, but he has his comms tracker."

"Then let's go." Manny turned and headed back to the shuttle at a fast clip. They roared out off the planet and docked on the *Annihilation*.

Gill was right behind him, jostling Slone on his shoulder. He set Slone down and strapped him in for takeoff. They roared off the planet and docked on the *Annihilation*.

Once they got to the ship, Gill handed Slone off to a medic and went to the bridge. He watched as Manny keyed in the information.

"They aren't far right now, but it looked like... Fuck, they just warped."

"In an Alliance ship? How is that possible?" Disbelief coloured Gill's voice.

"No idea, but we'll have to leave the *Annihilation* here and take the *Franklin*," Scott reasoned.

"Good call. Manny, take the *Annihilation* to Alliance headquarters and let the Commandant know our status. I'm taking my troops with Colonel Winchester so we can get the Captain back. Advise the Commandant that Alice Cole is once again behind it and we are going in guns hot. If he needs to get a hold of me, he knows where to reach me. Let's go." Gill turned to gather his men. "Scott, I'll meet you on the *Franklin* in five."

* * * *

The *Franklin* was in space, but Gill was impatient. Manny had given them the code and the tracker was up. They'd found the signal once they'd jumped. It was actually pretty easy to follow it. Thank God. He'd been worried they'd lost them. Scott had made the educated guess that Alice was on her way to Alto.

It didn't make sense, but it wouldn't because the woman was off-her-rocker crazy. They'd been so close to having normal again he'd let his guard down. He should have known better. It was always a fight and he was getting soft. Who knew what Rico was going through right now or even why he'd been taken. From what Scott had said, he could figure out the Nancy situation, but Rico? He might be better leverage, but for what? And why Alto? Scott had said it was a planet far away from the consortium. That was one of the reasons it didn't have inhabitants, but that hadn't bothered the people from Earth. They just wanted a place to settle before heading home and reporting what was going on. They weren't ready to leave when Alice had made her distress call.

At least he'd be able to see where his new home might be, if things worked out. He wondered what the Alliance would do and if they would join this consortium. But that was a worry for another day.

He paced the room he'd been given, but he couldn't settle down. Scott had said, even with warp, it would take about a week or more to get to Alto. He knew a direct way and they were taking it, hoping to beat Alice's ship.

Gill had been in contact with the Commandant and they were trying to work out how she'd got the Alliance ship to make the warp jump. They didn't have much time because communications had gone down after they'd left Earth's orbit. There was no way to get in touch with the planet anymore. They were on their own.

A beep alerted him that someone was at his door.

"Enter."

Scott walked in. "I know how she did it. The crew member who helped her gave her our ship's specs and she reworked them on the Alliance ship. We'll make sure that we get those to the Alliance technicians so the fleet can prepare for the move."

"That's great. The Commandant will be happy. Now we just need to get our people back and get this over with."

"I'm tired, Gill."

"Me too, Scott. Once this is finished I'm taking Rico on vacation. We need time to get to know each other."

"What do you mean? I thought you were partners."

Gill laughed. "I was as shocked as you when he said that. We met a year ago. He walked into the place I was working and we flirted a little bit, but didn't really talk until the day that first shot was fired. We didn't see each other until the plans were made to get your cooperation. I want more time with him and that bitch better not take that away from me." Gill sat down hard on the bed and cradled his head in his hands.

The bed sank lower. Scott sat beside him and squeezed his shoulder. "We'll find them."

"I'm just worried in what shape we'll find them."

"Me too. I didn't know how unstable she'd become. I should have checked into it before I started all of this shit."

"I think it's honourable how you tried to help a friend. It was feasible…what she said happened. And you were away for a really long time. You didn't know. It's not like you could get news all the way out here. Earth didn't have the communications capabilities, they still don't. We were too busy digging out after the flood to worry about that. The administration that knew about you was completely gone, as well as any data pertaining to the expedition. Maybe that's something we can pick up from this consortium. Who knows? I don't like being so far away from solid ground. How did you do this with no destination in mind?"

"Blind faith, I guess. It was easier with Nancy by my side. We did it that way on purpose. Couples were allowed to go on the trip to help with loneliness. Not that single people couldn't come. We had a few of them. Things are different now. In my heart Earth was home…until now. Now I can't wait to get back to Alto…with Nancy."

The computer pinged. "Colonel Winchester, your presence is requested on the bridge."

Scott looked at Gill. Gill shrugged. They both left the room.

"Sir, we have news. There's a ship dead in space in front of us. We believe it is the one Alice escaped on."

"Have you tried hailing them?"

"Not yet."

"Good. We need a plan." Scott looked to Gill.

"I have one." Gill grinned. It was time to pull out his invisibility suit. He rubbed his hands together in glee. It was about time he got to field-test it.

Chapter Fourteen

"Code Red. Hull breach," the computer repeated over and over.

Rico grinned.

Alice slapped him.

"What're you smiling at?" She hit him again.

He still didn't stop grinning. He knew what that sound meant. The cavalry had just shown up and he wouldn't give the bitch the satisfaction of knowing what was about to come.

"Go find out what the computer is about and why the hell have we stopped?"

Her minion scurried away to do her bidding.

"What's wrong, Alice? Things not going the way you want them to?"

She growled at him. "You shut up."

"Sorry, my dear, I can't shut up and tell you what you want to know." He smirked at her, knowing it would only fuel her fire.

Rico wasn't disappointed. He wanted to keep her as focused on him as he could because he didn't want her to go after Nancy.

"Ma'am, the ship has stalled. We're still holding space, but I don't know for how long. We didn't have time to do the necessary repairs needed for the long haul. We're still a week away from Alto. What should we do?" The guy all but wrung his hands.

"And the announcement?"

"We thought it might be because of the stall, but we sent someone down to check it out."

"Good, let me know what you find out." She waved him away.

"And the stall?"

"Get the fuckin' engineer on it. Do I have to do everything myself?" Alice was livid.

Rico just watched the interaction and wondered how long it would take Gill to get to him. It couldn't be much longer and the whole crew was freaked out by Alice. They wouldn't put up much of a resistance. They would probably be relieved to get rid of her.

"Well, it's been nice, Alice."

"What are you on about?"

"We're going to die out here once the oxygen is depleted if you can't get this hunk of junk up and running again, then what will you do? You'll never be in control. You should just let me go now," he continued to bait Alice.

"I'm going to rule the world. It might not be Earth, but it'll be mine."

Rico snorted. "You can't even get your ship there. How's that working out for you?"

"Shut your fucking mouth." She drew back her fist and hit his face.

A light blossomed behind his eye. Shit, she hit hard. Nancy had sat quietly through the whole ordeal and he hoped she'd keep it up.

The computer blared again. Alice swore and left the room.

"Why do you keep antagonising her?" Nancy whispered as if she was afraid to speak out loud.

"I'm trying to keep her away from you. This is the best way. And we should be out of here soon." He didn't elaborate just in case Alice had the room wired for sound. "Just keep sitting real still like and pretend you aren't there. Don't say anything that might set her off. I'll keep her off balance. Okay?"

"I don't like it…but all right."

"Good."

Now that he had that settled they waited for what would happen next in silence. Rico still worked on his bonds. His wrists were raw, but it was worth it. He'd like to be out of the rope before Gill showed, but he didn't know if he had enough time.

Before he knew it, Alice was back.

"No need to worry your pretty head. We'll be back under way within the hour. Now where were we? Oh, that's right." She hauled her hand in and hit him in the same eye.

His head was forced back with the impact and struck the chair. He was bound to have a concussion after all of this. His face now throbbed in time with his head. Alice had dropped something by the door when she'd walked in. He was almost afraid to find out what it was. He prayed Nancy wasn't at her breaking point yet because he expected her to call a halt to this any minute and that would be dangerous. He could take the blows better than she would be able to.

Alice left and bent down by the door picking up a pipe of some kind.

Fuck, this is going to hurt.

Rico braced himself. He had no idea where she'd swing first. He hoped like hell it wasn't his head because he wasn't sure how much more of that he could take. He didn't have to worry. She swung and hit his thigh. Nancy whimpered and he hoped like hell Alice hadn't heard it, but she did. She grinned and changed direction with the pipe. Nancy wasn't going to be able to handle that. Rico rocked the chair until it fell backward. He was able to roll over and knock Alice on her ass. He drew back and headbutted her.

Not his best idea, but he didn't have a lot of body parts he could use. His hands and feet were tied to the fucking chair. He rolled out of the way and the weight from his body cracked the chair. His hands were still tied together, but not on the chair. He wiggled around until he could hit the bottom of the chair against the bed, but Alice started to move. He couldn't have that. She still had the pipe.

He lifted his hips up, raising his legs in the air and bringing them down hard on to her body. A crack and his legs were free. Alice stopped moving. Good. He stood, but was off balance, his feet still tied together.

"Is she dead?" Nancy said softly.

Rico almost missed it. "I don't know, but I'm not going to check right now. We have to get out of here." He sat on the bed and got his hands from behind his back and put his legs on the edge so he could work the knots with his fingers. Now that he could see what he was doing it was easier and his legs were free in no time.

The walk to Nancy was wobbly, but he made it.

"I'm going to untie your hands first so you can get to mine, then we'll get your feet and be out of here."

Nancy whimpered and her eyes widened. Alice had to be awake. Damn, that didn't last long. Without taking his eyes off Nancy he kicked back, knocking Alice off balance. Before she had a chance to get back up he tackled her to the floor. She swung again and damn if she didn't hit the same fucking eye. It was going to be black and blue for sure. They rolled over and over. She pinned him down and went for a choke hold. Rico grabbed her hands and yanked them away from his throat. With a shift, she was back underneath him and that was when the door opened. He looked up and smiled. Gill. He was wearing a skin tight white body suit and holding a hood in his hands. His feet and hands were even covered in the material.

"You foolin' around on me? I didn't think you liked girls."

"You big goof. Ump." Rico dodged Alice's hand and pinned it down to the ground. "You're lucky I'm so very happy to see you." He looked down at Alice, "Damn it, stay still!" He glanced back up at Gill. "She won't be down for long and Nancy is still tied up. What are you wearing?"

Gill looked down at himself and grinned at Rico. "My clocking suit. Sweet, huh? Now — we need to get off this ship and get all these people over to the *Franklin*. The warp took everything out of the ship and whatever they're doing to fix it has started a reaction, the engine is about to blow. From what I can tell they were in a hurry and skipped a few steps." Gill cut the ropes from Rico's hands as he talked.

"Okay, you get Nancy and I'll take care of Ms Sunshine here. Did you alert the crew on board?"

"That's what took me so long. I had to convince them it wasn't a viable option to stay here. Scott has us hooked together for now, but he'll have to drop this ship soon or go explode too. So, hurry."

"I'm ready, what's taking you so long?" Rico had never been so happy to see another human being in his life. He'd thought that honour had been held when he'd laid eyes on Gill for the second time, but this was even better. Gill had saved him.

"Okay, I've got Nancy, let's go."

Rico followed Gill off the ship. They got in line behind the crew from the ship. There weren't many people there and they looked eager to leave.

"Ship's core to explode in T minus five minutes. Code Red. Evacuate in an orderly fashion." A computer voice droned on.

"Fuck, we have to hurry this along. All right, people, let's hustle." Rico shifted Alice on his shoulder.

Gill had just stepped through the bridge onto Scott's ship when Alice woke up. She pushed at him and he lost his balance. He slipped and she dropped to the ground. He reached for her, but she kicked him away. Gill was there and pulled him onto the ship. Rico reached out.

"Grab my hand."

Alice grinned and shook her head. The doors closed. He would never forget the look of insanity on her face as long as he lived. Gill was dragging him away as the bridge shut off and started retracting into the ship. It was close, but they were behind the seal and detached in enough time to watch Alice's ship explode with her still on board. She'd known what was about to happen and had seemed happy about it. It rocked the *Franklin* but it pushed them away. The force of the blast knocked Rico into Gill's arms. They must have warped because the flames disappeared into the blackness of space.

Chapter Fifteen

It had been two days since the incident with Alice. Rico was having nightmares and there was nothing Gill could do about it. At least not yet. They were being debriefed today and had a meeting set up with Scott and the Commandant. The negotiations would start on the evacuation. He knew Scott would be happy when it was over and he could go home.

He looked over at Rico. His eye was black, blue and purple and he had a concussion from all the blows to his head. The first night he'd had to stay in sick bay. Last night they had held each other. A few times he'd had to soothe Rico back to sleep.

The Commandant entered the room and both he and Rico stood up.

"Sit down and start filling me in."

"Yes, sir." Rico informed the Commandant of the goings on, letting him know about the other planet and Nancy's kidnapping before he turned the debriefing over to Gill.

"Once we realised Captain Clark had been taken we found the comm and found out Alice had warped. We knew we couldn't take the *Annihilation* so Colonel Winchester loaned us his ship so we could get our people back. We ran into Alice's ship, dead in the water, so to speak. We got everyone off and came home."

"I'm happy everyone is safe. And your wife, Colonel?" The Commandant turned to look at Scott, giving him his full attention.

"She is good, and resting on our ship. I wanted to thank you for speaking to me about our forces joining the Alliance. I think it will be beneficial to us all. My battalion can help get your ships warp-ready and by the end of the month we can start evacuating. Alto is a great planet and I think there is room for everyone. We also have other planets people can explore once we get everyone off Earth. As Captain Clark stated, I have a contact with the coalition that I'll make sure you have access to so the Alliance can thrive in space."

"Thank you, Colonel. It saddens me that it took so long to get here, but I'm happy that we are. I think this will be a smooth transition and hope you'll continue to be an ambassador between your people and ours."

Scott stood and nodded at the Commandant. "Thank you, sir. I would be happy to facilitate that."

"Good. I know that Alto is yours. Once we get people settled we'll start exploring to find a home base for the Alliance."

"Again, thank you, sir. If you'll excuse me, I'm going to check on my wife."

"By all means. We'll set up an appointment later in the week."

Scott turned and left, leaving him and Rico alone with the Commandant.

"Now that those formalities are out of the way I want to commend the two of you for going above and beyond in your duties. The council has got together and made a few decisions. You are now looking at the Commandant in Charge and the two of you will become my right- and left-hand men, both of you Commandants. Clark, you'll be in charge of the space programme and our liaison with the coalition. You did a wonderful job talking to Winchester and getting him on board."

"But...sir..."

Walker didn't let Rico finish. "I know what you're going to say and it doesn't matter that he was going to come in on his own. They way you handled the situation shows us you're the man for the job. As for you, Carter, you'll be the Commandant in charge of our ground troops. You showed great initiative in gathering them together to save Clark."

"There's something else you should know, sir." Rico cleared his throat before continuing. Gill knew what he was going to say and he held his breath. "Gill... Commandant Carter and I are...partners."

Now it was out there. They couldn't take it back. Not that he wanted to. He was happy to be Rico's partner in every way.

"Yes, you do work well together and you'll need to, to keep things running smoothly."

"That's not exactly what I meant, sir. We're *partners*." Rico took Gill's hand in his.

"Oh! Oh! Well, that's not a problem for us if it isn't for you. Once we find a planet to settle on you'll both be stationed there anyway to oversee training. You'll have to find people you trust to keep at your side. Things are going to open up and change for us once we leave Earth. We need to gather people close. The first thing I want the two of you to do is uncover who was working with Alice. We need to nip this rebellion in the bud. We can't have this kind of distraction as we prepare to leave. The two of you have the rest of the day off. You can report to headquarters tomorrow to start on that. Clark, once Winchester has his crew updating our ships, I want you to be a part of that."

"Yes, sir."

"Good day, gentlemen. Until tomorrow."

Gill stood and so did Rico. When the door had shut they both collapsed.

"It's so very surreal, isn't it?" Rico turned to looked at him.

"Yes, it is. I don't want to be *in charge* of anything." Gill laid his head on the table.

Rico laughed. "You'll do just fine."

"Ugh."

"Do you want to go to the *Annihilation*?"

"Yes, I just have a room in the barracks. I kind of feel at home on the ship."

"You'd better get used to it. I have a feeling that's going to be a base of operations for the foreseeable future." Rico stood and held out his hand. Gill took it and followed him out of the door. He'd follow Rico anywhere, even across the galaxy. Their love would only grow stronger. He hoped. They'd have a lot of time to find out as they prepared for a new life in a new world. Who knew an ex-cop turned bakery worker would be in charge of the ground forces for all of the Alliance? Not him, that was for sure. But Rico? He was made to be in charge and, in a few years, he could see his lover in charge of the whole kit and caboodle.

"You coming?"

"Right behind you, always."

They made a pit stop to check on Nancy. The four of them had grown closer over the last couple of days. Living through an adventure like that, they'd had to.

"You guys hungry?" Nancy asked as they entered the temporary quarters the Alliance had housed the couple in.

"I could eat." Gill rubbed his stomach.

"You're always hungry."

Gill leered at Rico and raised his eyebrows. Rico just laughed.

"So what happened after I left?" Scott sat down at the table with a plate.

Rico and Gill followed suit.

"You're now looking at two Commandants. Gill here is in charge of the ground crew and I'm in charge of the fleet."

"Congrats!" Scott slapped Rico on the back.

"I'll be working closely with you as we upgrade the ships and I'll also be the go-between with the coalition so we'll be working closely together."

"That is a huge relief for me. I like you, Rico. You too, Gill. It'll make the transition much easier for all of us."

After that there was a lot of small talk. It was a nice evening with friends, but Gill was ready to be home with Rico. Things were about to get crazy again and they needed some time for just the two of them.

"Thanks for dinner, guys. We'll see you later." Rico put his plate in the sink. Nancy stood and gave him a kiss on the cheek.

"Thank you." She squeezed his arm before moving on to Gill. "You too." She kissed Gill on the cheek.

Scott walked them to the door.

"Things are about to change. I'm happy that you two will be a part of it. It eases my mind considerably."

"I'm happy you hailed us that day and we could become friends." Rico pulled Scott to him and hugged him, patting his back. "Now get back to your wife. The next couple weeks are going to be nuts."

Gill and Rico walked hand in hand to the *Annihilation*. It really was a great name for a warship, but the only thing being annihilated was Gill's heart, and he couldn't be happier. Even through the crazy, he was happy with fate. He looked forward to many years with Rico.

Epilogue

Ten years later…

Rico paced one way and he watched as Gill paced the other. He thought they'd both have nerves of steel after setting up the Alliance and evacuating the population of Earth into unknown space. But this— this was much worse. Well, maybe not, depending on how he looked at it.

"What's taking so long?" Gill chewed on his thumb and had a wild look in his eyes.

"These things just—take time. Right? What the hell do I know? I've never been through this before."

"Well…go find out or something. This waiting is killing me."

"You and I both know that babies come in their own time," Rico tried to reassure Gill.

"But this is *our* baby and it's been too long. What if something happened?" Gill stopped and had a look of horror on his face.

"If something had happened they would have been out here already." Rico went to Gill and pulled him into his arms.

Once things had settled down he had talked to Gill about children. His mother's nagging had helped and Gill loved Rico's mom. Once Anne Marie said she wanted grandbabies Gill had been on board.

Of course, now the reality of the situation was setting in they were both a mess. Rico could make men tremble with a stare, but somehow he didn't think that would work with a kid. What had they been thinking? It was going to be tiny and helpless and what if they had to go off planet or something?

We should have thought about that before now!

The Alliance had settled on a planet not far from Alto. The consortium had let them join with minimal fuss. The Alliance had control of the system that included Alto and five other planets. There we always exploring for more planets. Who knew how big the Alliance would be in another ten years. Rico and Gill lived on Prime, where they'd set up the headquarters for the Alliance. The *Annihilation* was the flagship of the Alliance and Manny was now the captain. Rico was happy with that decision—it kept him at home now, which was why he and Gill had thought having a child now would be a good idea.

Scott was still in charge of Alto and each planet had what they were calling division chiefs. He and Nancy were due for a visit soon with their children.

"Both of you boys sit down, you're giving me a headache." Anne Marie waved them over.

Gill hurried to her side. Rico just shook his head and sat down.

"I'm sorry, Anne Marie—it's just so... I don't know...big."

"Well, it doesn't get any smaller, but I'll be here to help. Worrying won't help matters. I'm sure the doctors will be out soon." Anne Marie patted Gill's leg.

Thanks to some genetic altering the baby would have both his and Gill's genes. He didn't know all of the science behind it, but the baby would be his and Gill's — completely. The egg donor preferred to remain anonymous. That was the only reason neither of them was in the room with her. Despite all the advances in medical science it was still better to have a baby incubated with the mother. They hadn't gone the artificial uterus way other couples had because it just didn't seem natural. The gene splicing was enough for them both. They hadn't picked a designer baby, but had let nature do what it would.

"Commandant Carter, Commandant Clark, I'd like to introduce you to your son." A nurse came through the doors with a bundle wrapped in her arms.

"He's so tiny." Gill hovered over the nurse, his finger poised to touch.

The nurse moved to hand the baby to Rico, but he backed away. "What if I hurt him?"

"Don't be silly, son. Take your baby. Have the two of you thought of a name?" His mom cooed at the baby.

Rico shifted him around, but he started to cry. Gill took the baby from his arms and rocked him back and forth. Rico blinked — where was his worrier? It seemed he still had more to learn about the love of his life.

"Erik Ricardo Carter."

"Wait — what? I thought it would be Erik Gilliland Clark?" Gill looked confused but continued to rock the baby back and forth.

Rico's mom just beamed at him.

"Well, I was thinking it was time we made it official. We've been so busy we haven't had much us time and now we have a baby and I think we should all go by Carter. Maybe we'll have another baby and we can name him Clark Gilliland Carter, well, if it's another boy."

Gill smiled and walked towards him with the baby. He slung an arm around Rico and there they were, his family. Rico knew how important family was to Gill and how he'd lost his family in the flood, so it meant more to him to have his name carried on. Rico still had his mom, a tangible reminder of who he was and where he'd come from.

"When can we take him home?" Gill looked at the nurse.

Rico had almost forgotten she was there. He pushed the blanket aside so he could look at Erik's fingers and toes. He thought he was supposed to count them. Their son was perfect and, if he wasn't mistaken, he looked just like Gill.

"We'll keep him here overnight just to make sure everything is all right. We have a family room set up down the hall so you can stay with him if you'd like."

"We wouldn't be anywhere else," Gill assured her.

"Give me my grandbaby."

He'd wondered how long it would be until his mom took control of the baby. They'd better have more quick or he'd be spoilt before they knew it.

"I do believe I heard we have a wedding to plan." Anne Marie was walking away from them with the baby, following the nurse.

Rico hurried up his steps, dragging Gill with him.

"Um—Mom? It probably won't be a big affair. Right? Back me up here, Gill."

"Oh, I don't know..."

"Gill!"

His mom was chuckling and turned to wink at him. Life would never be dull in his family now he had two people to talk out of a big drawn-out wedding and to convince that the Commandant could say a few words and it would be official.

He knew he was kidding himself. It was going to be a grand affair, but he was really too happy to fight it.

* * * *

A few decades later…

James Rodrick closed the journal he'd been reading. He'd had so many things wrong. His partner Alphonse Carter's great-great-grandfather had been a wonderful guy. It was too bad he'd passed away because James would have loved to have met him and it sounded like Alphonse was a perfect blend of his ancestors with his grey eyes and blond hair. He wondered if Gilliland had had a journal and whether Alphonse could get his hands on it. The history that had established the Alliance was very interesting. Now he knew why Earth was off-limits, but he'd bet the planet could sustain life again after all this time.

He had an in with the head of the Alliance. Maybe it was time to use it to his advantage and take a crew exploring for his next vacation. As it was, he was setting up his ship so it could be the command centre for Alphonse. They felt it best he not stay in the same spot because of all the treason going on. The Alliance had got too big for its own good and it was time to clean house. Now, instead of a solar system, they were in charge of a galaxy and more, with everyone reporting to the Alliance. James wanted to know more about the consortium as well and why it had allowed the Alliance to take over control. He didn't remember learning about a hostile takeover, but what was it people said? The winner wrote the history books.

James got out of his chair and carefully removed the disk and set it down on the desk in his quarters. He might have hated the Alliance for a long time, but, after meeting his lover and reading about his great-great- grandfather, James had a new perspective.

It was getting late and he wondered where Alphonse was. Maybe he was putting his new office together. They'd finally cleared one of the living spaces up so he'd have a private area for his business dealings with the Alliance. They were orbiting Prime before they took the *Reward* to deep space and poked around for a bit.

He was getting hungry, so he went in search of his lover. Alphonse might be in need of a break too. Maybe Alphonse knew more about the consortium. If nothing else, he could ask Alphonse if he had any news on his brother, Angel. He'd gone missing after helping take out a threat against the Alliance. Alphonse was worried and, in turn, so was James.

James found him in his office with his head in his hands.

"Babe, what's up?" James walked over to the desk and began rubbing Alphonse's shoulders.

Alphonse reached up and grabbed James' hands, giving them a squeeze.

"They found Angel's ship, but it was abandoned. No signs of life. There was some blood found, but the DNA matched to Frank Morgan. The ship looked like it had been ransacked. That could mean one of two things — that they left in a hurry or someone took them by force."

"That was the informant, right? The one Angel left with?"

"The very same. If he's gone under, we'll never find him. If he's dead…"

"Don't think that way, Alphi." James wrapped his arms around Alphonse's shoulders and kissed his cheek. "He'll come home when he's ready. Maybe there was more to what happened than we know."

"You're right, but this fuckin' sucks, Jimmy."

James smiled against Alphonse's neck. He'd hated that nickname once upon a time, but now he cherished the times Alphonse used it.

"Let's go eat dinner."

"I'm not hungry."

Was that a pout he heard in his lover's voice? He needed to get Alphonse in a better mood.

"You might not be, but I am and I want the company. Come talk to me about the Alliance of old."

"You must have finished Great-Great-Granddad's journal."

That was a bit better and now they were on a subject James could talk about all night. He loved history.

"I did and I want more. Did your other great-great-grandfather have a journal too?"

"Not that I know of. He wasn't the writing type."

"I want to know how the Alliance took over the consortium."

"I might be able to tell you about that, if you give me an incentive." Alphonse winked at him.

James laughed, happy that the mood had lightened a little.

"You know—we could always go look for your brother. It isn't like you're tied to an office and I don't have any cargo runs scheduled for a little bit. And, even if I did, we could work around it."

He shouldn't have brought the topic back around to Angel because he didn't want Alphonse sad, but he had to offer to help. If it had been his brother, Alphonse would have done the same.

Alphonse stood and turned into James' arms. James hugged him tight.

"I love you."

"I love you too, Alphi. Now let's go eat and talk about our plans to save your brother."

They walked to the mess hall to make plans. James just hoped he wasn't giving Alphonse false hope. He would move heaven and earth to find the brother of the man he loved.

"Sounds like a great plan to me. Now — about the consortium. There was some fighting within the organisation and the Alliance was in a position to take control. At least that's what I've gathered from family talks. Part of the consortium merged with the Alliance and they gained power. The other half that was fighting disappeared. Never to be heard from again."

"Very interesting. I wonder where they went."

"We'll never know, will we? More puzzles for your brilliant brain to work on."

"You sweet-talker, you. Is this where I offer up my incentive? You've already given me the goods."

"Yep, now it's your turn to give it up."

"Sir, yes, sir."

The lighthearted banter was something he could deal with. They would get through this tough time together and hopefully, at the end of it all, Angel would be found. He had to be out there somewhere.

AVENGER

Dedication

To family and loving them no matter what—yes, this includes Joy and Ive um...and all my online family. Just goes to show you that not all family has to have blood ties.

Chapter One

Angel Carter couldn't believe his bad luck. It was supposed to be an easy undercover job. But he should have known by now that nothing in his life was ever easy.

"Buckle up, we're about to crash." Angel glanced at Frank Morgan—his inside man on the deep undercover job had gone all to hell. Frank looked rough. His stubble had stubble and there were circles under his eyes. His short dark hair sticking up every which way and the white of the bandage on his side stood out against his skin. Angel hadn't put a shirt on Frank. Angel licked his lips and he should've been ashamed of himself for being turned on when it appeared as if Frank was passed out from lack of blood.

He wasn't sure if Frank had even heard him, the man had been loopy from the drugs. Getting shot would fuck anyone up. Angel didn't know how he felt about Frank getting injured or why he felt the need to run when he should have stayed and helped his brother, Alphonse, but every instinct had screamed at him to get Frank and get off the planet. Now they were about to both go down in a hail of metal and fire. If the crash didn't kill them, the re-entry into Earth just might.

But he was out of options. He was going to the one place he should be safe. Earth had been abandoned for decades after it had almost been destroyed. Reports showed it was liveable again, but the Alliance was keeping it under wraps for now. They wanted to get hard data before letting people re-inhabit the place.

He hoped to hell the reports were right because in T-Minus twenty minutes he was going to find out, first-hand, just how good the air quality was. Angel leaned over and strapped Frank in, taking a moment to caress his cheek. Damn this attraction he had to Frank. It was going to get them both killed—if the ship didn't kill them first.

"Erik…where…what…?" Frank winced.

Angel wanted to apologise, but really…what could he say? It wasn't his fault Frank had been involved in a lot of bad shit that had come back to bite him on the ass.

"Frank, you shouldn't call me that."

And he shouldn't have said that. Frank knew Angel was undercover, but not his real name, and now there would be questions. He should have just left it alone. But no—they might die and he didn't want to lie. Damn it. His timing sucked, but he had a strong pull towards the criminal and he wanted him something fierce.

"Why? It's your name." Frank blinked at him—he still seemed a bit out of it.

"Not really."

Shit, shit, shit. Shut up, man!

"Huh?" Now Frank looked confused on top of being hurt.

"I'll explain later." Angel tried to wave it off, but he'd got to know Frank somewhat during the investigation and the man wasn't going to give up.

"Just explain now." Frank bit down on his lip as the ship hit a bad run of turbulence.

They were going down fast. The outer shields were burning as they entered the atmosphere. Out of his peripheral vision he could see a blue glow—flames coming from somewhere. It didn't look good. He had to switch to manual. The computer shut down—he wasn't sure if that was from the heat inside or if it'd been hit.

"My full name is Angel Erik Carter. You knew I was undercover. I try to stick as close to my name as possible. I used Erik Angel so people still call me Angel—well, except you. Makes it easier. Of course, now you know my last name and you can't say anything. Not yet. There are too many—"

Shit, Frank had passed out. His head listed to the side. Frank needed help and Angel wasn't sure he'd be able to do much good with only basic medical skills. Fuck. Frank should be in a base hospital. Angel's head was all screwed up. He needed to call Alphonse or his dad. Someone had to be able to help him.

The ship began to beep at him. Angel needed to get his head back into the game before the ship was completely wrecked. If the trajectory was just right the craft would be salvageable. A landing in a body of water might work if his maps on board were up to date. Angel always fell behind in getting his ship upgraded and not much of Earth's terrain was known anymore, at least not by him. Their scientists hadn't been out there for a really long time as far as Angel was aware. Of course, science wasn't his forte.

Angel took a quick glance at his passenger. Was Frank getting pale, and was that blood seeping out of the bandage? Landing on an unpopulated planet with a man who could be dying, he'd been in worse situations, right? He could do this. *Double damn.*

The ship shook so badly Angel feared it would fall apart. Land was in view and there wasn't a body of water in sight. Of course not. That would've made things easier for him. Angel pushed a couple of buttons and reversed thrusters, engaging his emergency landing gear. The *Avenger* made a god-awful screeching sound. Angel put up a quick prayer as the ship slammed into the ground. He jerked forward, his safety harness biting into his neck. His head hit the console and bounced back against his seat. He blinked as something warm and sticky slid down his face.

He used a hand to wipe it off. Blood. Just what he needed. What else could go wrong? Angel took a moment to collect his thoughts and catalogue any injuries he might have. He wasn't feeling so hot and his head was spinning from the blow, but that seemed to be the extent of the damage to his person. Angel fumbled with his buckle but couldn't seem to undo it—his hands kept slipping. He wiped them on his jeans.

An alarm buzzed through the ship. That should have happened sooner—like, on impact. His ship was fucked. Damn it. Smoke was starting to fill the bay. He needed to get up and see how Frank was.

"Come out with your hands up."

Well, fuck.

Angel shouldn't have said anything about shit getting worse, because when you put that out there — things went tits up. Earth shouldn't be populated. Who were these people? Everyone was supposed to have been evacuated and there had been no reports of inhabitants. Frank wasn't budging and there was no getting out of whatever was going to happen. Angel sighed and took off his harness. He rubbed his shoulder and moved closer to Frank.

"I need you to wake up, Frank."

Frank just grunted.

"Damn it, Frank, we've got a situation here. I need you to wake up."

He had no idea how long the people outside would give him before they stormed the ship. He needed Frank up and about. Angel hoped they had some sort of medical facility nearby.

Angel ran his hands over Frank's chest and down his side, stopping at the bandage. It looked like the blood was flowing again but Angel knew it shouldn't have been. Not if a normal laser had been used. It wasn't a graze.

Frank moaned and something started banging against the hull of the ship. Angel shifted away from Frank and had to do something he usually didn't do — hope for the best. He strode to the door, took a deep breath, pushed the button to open it, then held his hands up.

"Hey there, neighbour, got a cup of sugar I can borrow?"

* * * *

What the fuck?

Frank groaned. He hurt all over. What was the last thing he remembered? He'd been at his boss' place and things went to shit. He had been helping a hot undercover Alliance agent stop a coup. That's when things got fuzzy. He'd—shit, he'd been shot. He jack-knifed up and clutched at his side. He almost fell back down again but managed to stay sitting and not throw up. It was a close call.

"Fuck, fuck, fuck." Frank managed not to yell the words, but not by much.

"Shh. It's okay."

Who was—oh, Erik, but not Erik. He remembered a bit of the crash. Where were they?

"Er—Angel?" Frank glanced towards where the voice was coming from.

Angel sat on a cot against a wall with his head in his hands.

"Yep. Welcome back." Angel looked up and winked at him.

There was a gash on his head. He didn't remember Angel getting hurt, not that he had much of a memory of events. Had Angel...carried him out of the building? Had they run? He had so many questions.

"Where are we?" Frank pressed at his side. It fuckin' hurt.

"Would you believe, Earth?" Angel shrugged.

"No, fuckin' way." Frank peered at Angel in disbelief.

"Yes fucking way." Angel laughed.

"It was deserted—forever ago."

Frank had heard the stories growing up. How the people had been forced from the planet because of a war. It was uninhabitable. They shouldn't be here. It was dangerous.

"Not so much anymore."

"Huh?" Frank had a hard time wrapping his head around everything.

Frank looked around. They were in some kind of structure. Were those — bars?

"It seems someone took over Earth while the Alliance wasn't paying attention."

"How is that possible?"

"Well — we'd heard some rumblings of someone trying to take over. We've been a bit preoccupied. How are you doing?"

"I was shot. How do you think I'm doing? So, we're on Earth, but — where exactly?"

"My maps aren't up to date so I'm unsure. But right now — we're in a jail cell."

"Fuck, I was trying to avoid that." Frank had to chuckle at the irony of the situation.

"Yeah, well, they patched you up a bit, so that's something."

"Have you talked to them yet?"

"Nope. They…ah…might not have enjoyed my greeting."

Frank just shook his head. He didn't know a lot about Angel, but he did know he was a smart ass. Usually he was more mysterious, which had his old boss, Vincent, in an uproar. It was also something that had always drawn him to the man. Now was not the time to think about his attraction.

"I don't even want to know. How are we getting out of here?"

"I have a plan." Angel stood and walked to the bars blocking the exit.

Frank saw a toilet in the corner. It really was an old-fashioned cell, but it wasn't as dirty or smelly as he would have imagined a cell on Earth to be. These people had to have been there for a while. It seemed...newish with grey walls. No cracks or leaks, but the damn water in the toilet was constantly running. The cot he was on was surprisingly soft. He wondered what else was around to explore and if it was as nice as the cell. He hoped it would be nicer.

"Of course you do." Frank winced when he tried to stand and decided against it.

"What's that supposed to mean?" Angel turned back around to look at Frank.

"I don't know — but your last plan got me shot."

"So, not my fault." Angel grasped the bars and shook them.

It didn't appear as if they'd moved.

"And so not the point."

"This is true. Okay, we need to — shit, someone's coming."

Angel returned to his cot and stretched out like he had nothing better to do.

"What are you — ?"

"Lay back down and close your eyes."

"Why — ?"

"Just fucking do it!" Angel glared at him.

Sure, just a stroll in the park. Frank, I need your help. Frank, if you turn evidence you'll be safe. Trust me, Frank. He closed his eyes. His mamma had told him a life of crime would lead to trouble. All he had wanted was a quick buck, not the takeover of the Alliance. And Vincent, his boss, had gone a little nuts. He was done with the whole thing. Maybe he'd stay here and disappear. Obviously the Alliance was looking the other way.

A creak alerted him to the door opening. He wanted to open his eyes but feared what he'd see. Was the planet even stable? What kind of effects would long-term exposure have on the people if it wasn't stable?

The air didn't seem bad in the cell, but that was inside. They could have purified air in the buildings. What did he know?

Maybe if he'd asked more questions before this, he wouldn't be in this mess. He was always following his dick. Only reason he'd been with Vincent to begin with was because his boyfriend at the time had talked him into it. Frank was a loyal guy and couldn't just leave after his boyfriend had dumped him. At the time Vincent had been a solid character then he had gone all crazy.

"The commander would like to see you." Frank assumed that was their guard talking.

"Are you asking or telling?"

Angel sounded calm, but Frank couldn't believe he was playing with these people. They had no idea what they'd dropped into. He was either fearless or stupid. Frank was going with stupid.

"Get your ass up and come with me."

Frank opened his eyes just a tad to see who had been speaking. The guy was huge—and was he...purple? What the hell? Maybe he was hallucinating. Had they drugged him?

Angel didn't rush to the door, nor did he glance Frank's way. What was he supposed to do? Not like he could rush the big guy. There was no fucking way in the state he was in. They'd both end up dead. He'd like to get out of this whole fucking shit storm alive and maybe, not purple. He didn't know shit about science. All he knew was how to be an enforcer and right-hand man to a crime syndicate boss.

Frank watched helplessly as Angel was shoved out of the door.

Chapter Two

Voit Reno sat in his office and awaited the arrival of the crash victim. They'd had his ship towed to the mechanic bay. It was in bad shape and he didn't know if it was salvageable. Not that it mattered. He was too close to having his plans fall into place for something out of the blue like this to happen. He wondered if the Alliance was on to him.

The ship didn't look to be governmental. It was too small, but what did he know. They'd been off the grid for too long. He had a few inside men, but he didn't tap them too often. He didn't want them caught. It was time the Alliance went back to where it came from and what better way to accomplish this than to explore what they used to be? Earth had been good to them over the centuries. The Consortium should have done away with the Alliance when they'd asked for admittance and had slowly taken over. Not that he could fully blame the Alliance, the Consortium had suffered from infighting as any big organisation would, but they'd taken advantage of the political struggles.

Most wanted to give up and were happy to be on Earth. His right-hand man, Archer Tok, wanted to petition to join the Alliance. Voit wasn't sure and needed more convincing. For him—he felt it was time to hook up with the Consortium of old and show the Alliance what a true powerhouse was.

There was a knock on his door.

"Enter."

"Commander." Archer pushed the man into Voit's office.

"That'll be all, Tok."

His friend looked hesitant but left the room. He could tell that his friend and advisor wanted to say more, but he knew better then to undermine him in front of others. They'd been working together for too many years. He'd probably hear about it after the meeting, but so be it. He was hoping to make the guy comfortable so he'd talk.

"Please have a seat. I'm Commander Voit Reno. And you are?"

"Bored."

"Excuse me?" He couldn't have heard right. What kind of prisoner responded with that? Of course, he had heard about the greeting the man had given Voit's soldiers.

"Yeah—your cell leaves much to be desired. I'm used to better accommodation and a bed that isn't thin and rock hard. You should see about getting that fixed."

Voit smirked. Whoever the guy was, he'd sprawled out on the chair like he had every right to be there, his hands resting on his stomach, and he wasn't scared. His blond hair spiked all over like he'd ran his hands through it over and over. His silver eyes had a pinched appearance to them, but he was smiling like he was just here for a visit with an old friend.

"I'll see what I can do, but I still need to know your name and what you're doing here." Voit leant forward in his chair.

"Well—I could ask you the same questions."

Voit wasn't used to having the tables turned on him. He was the one in charge and people followed his orders.

"You could, could you? And why is that?"

What a cocky bastard. He almost admired him. Almost.

"Nobody is supposed to be here." He shrugged.

"And you know this how?" Voit sat back in his chair. This conversation was getting interesting. He wondered how much a space captain would know about Earth. The Alliance seemed to like to play things close to the vest. Was this a spy ordered to infiltrate the camps Voit had here on Earth? They'd repopulated about half of the Earth and they weren't giving it up.

"I'm not going to give away all my secrets, slick."

"I can see that. You're not giving up anything. Not even a name."

It was getting a little annoying and Voit was ready to throw him back into the brig no matter how interesting his prisoner was.

"I've always been told to give out name, rank and serial number." There was a shrug.

"Ah. So you are a military man."

"Maybe. Or could be I watch a lot of really old vids. You can call me Angel."

He had a pair of balls on him, that was for sure. Fucker. What was his game?

"That's all you'll give me? All right then. Why are you here?" Voit held in his sigh. He wasn't giving Angel the satisfaction of seeing his frustration.

"Hiding."

"From?"

"Does it matter?" There was Angel's cheeky grin again.

"Yes. Should I expect more craft to land?" That was what worried Voit the most. That someone from the Alliance would come before he was ready.

"No."

Angel had sounded positive about that, but it still didn't ease Voit's concerns.

"If you're running, how do you know?"

"No one would come to Earth. It's off limits." Angel had seemed to stress the last words, or was that his imagination?

"But you're here." Voit waved a hand at Angel.

"True." Angel nodded at him and pursed his lips like he was thinking.

"What were you expecting to find?"

"An empty planet to hide out on and relax for a bit. Nothing more." Angel shrugged.

"So you had no idea there were civilisations here? You could have landed in an Alliance stronghold." Voit rested his elbows on the desk and laced his fingers together, then tapped his lips. He was watching Angel closely to see if he would give anything away with his answer.

"Not to my knowledge, no. And I don't think you're Alliance." Angel cocked an eyebrow.

"And your—friend?" He'd ignore the Alliance comment for now.

"What about him."

"How were you planning on helping him with his injuries?"

"I was going to figure that out as I went along. I have a med kit, but won't say I wasn't happy you have better medical facilities. Are you a part of the Alliance?"

Now it was clear Angel was tense, waiting for an answer.

Very interesting.

"Would it matter if we were?" It was his turn to shrug.

"It might explain your presence on a planet that had been evacuated and barely able to support life. At least that's what I've been told. Bedtime stories, you know." Angel eased back into his chair.

He couldn't fool Voit, though, he still had a predatory look about him that he was clearly trying to hide. Voit wondered just what his story was. But that could wait. First they would go over the systems aboard the ship and see just what kind of vessel it was. They had the best hackers in the system.

"Let me just say that the planet is...inhabited and leave it at that. Once we know your true reason for being here, we'll have another chat. Until then, you'll have to remain in our cell. Once you've been cleared we can let you out." Voit pushed the intercom. "Tok, please escort our guest back to his room."

The door opened, but Voit kept his gaze on Angel. The man stood tall and followed Tok out of the door. He hoped this didn't mean the ends of his plans.

Tok was back in no time.

"Voit. I think we need to contact the Alliance."

"Not yet." Voit turned to look out of the window in his office.

"We can't keep fighting our ancestors' war." Tok stood close behind him. "And you should have let me stay in the room with you. What if he'd attacked? We have no idea who he is."

They might have been intimate at one time, but now they were just friends. It was better that way. Tok could keep him grounded.

"I need to know more about the Alliance before I trust our people in their care. History says we were pushed out by the Alliance. I have to find out the truth behind this." Voit rubbed at his tired eyes. "And—I was perfectly safe. I know you didn't step away from the door for a second, my old friend."

It sucked being in charge some days.

"You're right. I wasn't going to take a chance. And what if the Alliance did push the consortium out? That was the past. Things are different now." Tok moved even closer.

Voit knew Tok wanted more from him, but he just couldn't give him what he needed. Not now, maybe not ever.

"That may be, my *friend*, but I still have to be sure and I need to know who this Angel is. Let's go take apart a ship." Voit gripped Tok's shoulder and headed out of the door. They had things to do.

Fuck, fuck, fuck.

This was bad. Maybe worse than Angel'd originally thought. No way was this an Alliance planet. It couldn't be. He would have known about it, right? That would have been something important that his father would have told him in his briefings. And if they weren't—who were they? It would probably be a few hours before they stripped his ship and had an idea of who he was. Then what would happen?

And he'd dragged Frank into this mess. And why had he done that again? Because he wanted in the guy's pants. Damn it. He should never have left the planet and should've turned Frank over. Frank did have information that the Alliance needed to stop some of the gun and drug trafficking. And why was Angel falling for a criminal? He had the Alliance running through his blood. Hell, his great-great-grandfather had been one of the officers to help form the damn thing into what it was today.

His father was the Commandant in Charge for now. He was up for retirement soon. Angel would probably get the job but only because he didn't want to be the Commander in Chief. His brother would be great with that. If he was being honest with himself he didn't want his dad's position either. Not that it would matter if he died on Earth.

Frank was sleeping when he got back to the cell. He should've been relieved. Angel went closer and laid a hand against his forehead. Frank wasn't hot. That was a good thing. What was he going to do? He needed to find a way to get them out of this cell.

There weren't many options, no windows and on the walk to his jailer's office he hadn't noticed any doors that could lead outside—maybe beyond that would be something, but they'd still have to go past that door, and who knew if the guy would be inside. They would have to make it up on the fly. Usually he was good with that, but his fucking head hurt and Frank still wasn't one hundred per cent. And—yeah, most of the time he only had to worry about getting his ass out of a tight spot. He had never had a partner for a fucking reason.

"Angel?" Frank blinked up at him.

"Yeah, it's me." Angel knelt by the cot.

"You okay?" Frank sat up.

Angel helped him. "They didn't beat anything out of me if that's what you want to know, but it isn't looking good. I don't think they're Alliance and if they aren't — then who are they and how did they come to Earth?"

Frank swung his legs around and Angel shuffled forward on his knees. He licked his lips. They were in a fucked up situation He had to know. Angel edged forward and brushed his lips against Frank's. They were a bit chapped, but Angel didn't care. That little taste wasn't enough.

"What are you — ?"

Angel didn't let him get any further than that. He took Frank's lips again, putting his hands behind Frank's head so he couldn't move. He moaned when Frank opened his mouth and sucked his tongue in.

Frank jerked away. "Ouch. Fuck. Shit."

He leant back and wiped a hand down his face. He wouldn't apologise. If he could, he'd fuck Frank right then. Hell, he still might if Frank agreed.

"Your injury. You okay?"

"Yes, but what the hell was that?"

Angel shrugged. What could he say?

"We might die in here and — "

"So what, I'm fucking convenient?" Frank pushed him away.

"That could be it, but do you really think I'd take you off a planet where you had a deal set up if it wasn't more?"

"How am I to know what you're thinking? You're a fuckin' ninja assassin guy. A mystery wrapped in a stupid enigma. Yes, a dumb cliché in black leather." Frank rested his head on the bars.

Angel walked behind him and laid his head on Frank's back and controlled his chuckle, barely.

"A—what was that? Ninja assassin cliché in black leather?"

"Too much?" Frank's shoulder shook.

He sighed. "Maybe just a little. I'll tell you something—and I'm giving you my complete faith right here and right now."

"Maybe you shouldn't. I'm a bad bet, Angel." Frank still hadn't shifted away from the cell door.

Angel rubbed his hands down Frank's arms, soothing him as much as he could.

"You were turning over a new leaf. Things were going to change. I want to help you with that. Can I trust you?" Angel hoped he wasn't doing the wrong thing, but he knew after all was said and done, he was finished with undercover work. He was too old for it. Time to let the younger generation do what they could.

"I—yes. Yes you can."

"Good. That's—yeah…good. I'm—" It was harder than he had thought. He hadn't gone by his real title in so long. He turned Frank around so he could look into his eyes. "I'm Commandant Angel Erik Carter. My brother is Commandant Alphonse Carter. My dad is Commandant in Charge Robert Carter. My brother is about to be promoted to Commander in Chief of the Alliance."

Chapter Three

"Fuck." Frank closed his eyes.

"Well—if you're sure."

Frank opened his eyes and Angel winked at him.

"Bring on the jokes, funny man. If they find out who you are and they aren't Alliance, we're in a world of hurt, and you're thinking with your dick."

Angel eased a hand down between them and Frank didn't flinch. He knew what Angel would find.

"I'm not the only one thinking with their little head, Frank." Angel was almost taunting him.

"Sure, I want you more than I've wanted any other man, but we're in a situation here. We need a plan." He *could* think beyond his libido.

"That we do. That we do, but I'm all out of them. Right now I can only think about your lips and how good they'd look wrapped around my cock."

"And who says it'd be my lips?" Frank smirked but not for long.

Angel dropped to his knees. Frank couldn't look away, he wasn't—oh, yes he was. Angel unzipped his pants and pulled Frank's cock out. Everything else fled from Frank's mind. His side still hurt, but that warm mouth surrounding his dick deserved his full attention.

He ran his hands through Angel's hair, trying not to tug or thrust too hard. It had been so long. He'd been so worried with being a double agent he hadn't even taken time to think about his own pleasure. Frank's ass flexed and his whole body tensed. He was going to come any second.

"Angel, Ang, Ang...oh, fuck."

Teeth scraped his shaft and Angel's talented tongue soothed the burn. He stroked Frank's balls. Angel took him in deep—he nuzzled his nose into Frank's curls, then he swallowed. Frank's vision blurred and he screamed his release.

When he opened his eyes, Angel was standing right there. Frank dragged Angel closer. He wanted to taste himself on Angel. His cock was interested and tried to rise again, but it was too soon. Angel was still hard against his thigh. Frank went to edge down the cool bars, but his side wasn't going to let that happen.

"I got this." Angel stopped Frank from moving, but shifted back and grabbed his own shaft.

Frank licked his lips and couldn't look away. It was so hot watching Angel jack off. Frank pulled up his shirt so it wouldn't get in the way. Angel tugged on his balls and his hands raced over his length. It didn't take him long to lose his load all over Frank. Angel was panting and so sexy. Frank hadn't even seen him open his own pants. God, what would it feel like having that fat cock up his ass? Frank ran his fingers through the cooling cum on his stomach and sucked the salty goodness off them.

Angel moaned and took Frank's digits out of his mouth and put them in his own. Now it was Frank's turn to moan.

"I'm gonna fuck you."

"Here? Now?" Frank raised an eyebrow.

Angel nuzzled his head into Frank's neck. Licking and nibbling.

"No. As soon as we get out of here."

"And that would be?" Frank grabbed Angel's ass and rubbed their sensitive dicks together.

"In — five, four, three — "

What the hell is the crazy man doing now?

"What are you — ? Back away from the bars."

Frank turned to look behind him. Great, his ass was hanging out and some stranger was coming towards them. So very not cool, but not totally unexpected. They were prisoners and he had screamed pretty loudly when he'd come. It was bound to bring someone to investigate. He just hoped this hadn't been some plan Angel had concocted on the fly.

"Pull up your pants and get ready," Angel whispered before backing away.

He did as asked and turned to face the door.

"Do I need to separate you two?" the solider wanted to know.

Maybe he didn't realise they'd been fucking around.

"No need to do that. You could join."

Frank looked over at Angel and frowned. Or he did know? Just what was he up to and why was he flirting with the guard?

To Frank's surprise the bars opened. He moved away farther. This could end badly. They had no idea who these people were or how they felt about two men together. Or, the guy really could be coming in to join them. He wasn't sure how he felt about that. It might be better than a beating, but not by much.

Angel rushed the guard turned him around and put his arms around his throat, cutting off his air supply.

"Angel," Frank whispered.

"Shh, just grab the door."

The solider struggled a bit before he passed out. Angel stripped him and handed the clothes to Frank before holding onto the bars himself.

"He's more your size and I've been seen in the hallways. Make it quick."

Frank shook his head, but again did as asked. This could go very wrong. He hoped they wouldn't put out a shoot-on-sight order.

"Do you really think this is a good idea?" Frank struggled into the pants and buttoned up the shirt. "And please tell me you didn't just blow me so we could escape."

"No and no."

"What?" He couldn't believe Angel had calmly admitted he had no idea what he was doing. This was just great, but he was happy their sexual encounter had been more than a ploy to get the guard to come to them.

"No, this is not the best idea, but we have to get out of here before they find out who I am. I'm good ransom material if nothing else. No one knows I'm here and I'd kinda like to keep it that way until I can report in. The blow job was just a bonus—a really, really nice bonus."

Angel led him down a hallway, but Frank stopped him.

"If we have any hope of getting out of here, I need to lead. You're the prisoner, remember? And we need to make it quick before the guard is found."

"Right." Angel nodded and hung his head.

It was amazing how quick he could get into a role. No wonder he was an undercover operative. Frank had no idea where they might be going, but hopefully their luck would hold out.

Angel stared at Frank's ass as they hurried down the hallway. He wanted in and as soon as they found a place to hide he was going to fuck Frank until he couldn't walk. They hit a dead end and had to turn around. If they went the other way they were going to have to go past the commander's office.

That wouldn't be a good option, but they might not have another choice. He couldn't remember if there was a door before they got to the offices or not, but they were going to have to take their chances. There had been a window in the office and it looked out onto a small town square. Everything was green. He wondered just what part of the planet they were on.

"We have to turn around," Frank whispered.

"I know. We're going to have to hurry though because we'll be passing the commander's office."

"Fuck," Frank muttered.

"Yeah, tell me something I don't know."

"You're an ass?"

"Nope, know that too." Angel snickered.

He looked back to see Frank shaking his head, but he had a smile on his face. That was a good thing. Frank was holding onto his side. How could Angel have forgotten? The man was still injured. They'd fixed him up, but that didn't mean he wasn't in pain.

They turned around and headed the other way. They were getting closer to the office. If they were in some movie it would be time for the dramatic music to start playing, but they managed to get around it with no issues. *So far so good.*

There was a light coming from the right and he nudged Frank that way. It was hopefully an exit to the outside. Angel wondered how many people populated the planet and how far stretched out they were. He needed to contact his father. Someone had to know there were people here and gauge their risk to the Alliance. They already had too much in-house back-stabbing going on. Hopefully Alphonse had a handle on that and would have the house cleaned before Angel got back. No matter, they had to deal with this situation. To talk to these people and find out how they'd slipped under the Alliance radar.

Did the corruption go that far? How had things got so bad? It had to be because of how fast things expanded. How could you watch over a whole galaxy without some issues? They needed a stronger base of people they could trust.

That was the hard part—trusting people not to become corrupt.

The creak of the door pulled him out of his musings. He glanced around and there was no one in sight. He wasn't really sure what to expect when they got outside. From the books he'd read the place was crumbling, but not here. Buildings lined the streets. What they were for he didn't know, but they weren't dilapidated. It looked as if it was right out of a history book, but smaller than he'd imagined. Angel wondered how long they'd been on Earth to make it appear...whole and lived-in. Maybe the rest of the planet was worse off than this little town.

"This way." Frank tugged him along.

He had better stop daydreaming and get them someplace safe. He nodded and they ducked into an alley to avoid being spotted. He peered around to get his bearings and was still amazed with how good it seemed and how fresh the air was. It appeared like a town out of the Old West that his dad had made him watch a vid about and there were mountains in the distance. Maybe there was a cave they could get to. It would be better if he could find the ship, but it still required a lot of work. They had to buy some time.

"We have to get to the high ground before they put out a call that we've escaped. You think you can make it?"

"If you can, I can. Let's go." Frank gave him a firm nod.

"All right then, let's get to it."

"We should to find water and food somehow or we might as well stay here."

He needed to get his head out of his ass. He knew they wouldn't be able to hide out for long without supplies. Who knew how cold it would get? He didn't want to break out of the cell only to die from exposure.

"Okay, let's find shelter and when night falls I'll come back down and see what I can swipe."

They were going to have to go through some open territory, but if they hustled it they should be fine. Hopefully the commander would think they would hide out in town, but he didn't want to underestimate him. He had to look at this from all sides.

Frank was pale but seemed better than he had in days. Angel'd have to check the wound when they stopped for the night. Frank was still holding on to his side.

"Let me know if you have to stop, Frank."

"You know we're delaying the inevitable, right? We should get off this planet."

"No, not yet. We have to find out who these people are," Angel insisted.

"How do you propose we do that? We have no weapons and we're on the run. We don't even have anything to barter with." Frank turned and glared at him. His hands were on his hips and he had a mulish expression on his face.

Angel just wanted to kiss him, but they had more important things to talk about right then. He wasn't used to working with a partner and having to stop and explain himself. He just did what had to be done and managed to wiggle out of tight spots.

"We have information. I'll find out where the good commander sleeps and pay him a little visit." It really was as simple as that. He was good with threats and being ominous.

"Do you really think that's a good idea?"

"Nope." He grinned.

"Do you ever have any 'good' ideas?"

"Nope." This time Angel winked at Frank.

"You're so frustrating." Frank threw his hands up in the air.

"You're not the first one to say that and probably won't be the last."

"Why don't we stay in town if you're going to hunt him out?"

"It would be too easy for them to find us."

"You think? If I was trying to find someone who was escaping my first order would be to go into the hills. It's too easy."

"Too easy? To climb all the way up there?" Angel pointed.

"Yes. And there is no guarantee we'll even find shelter there."

"You're a real buzz kill, you know."

"Yep." Frank laughed.

And damned if Frank wasn't right. Angel turned back towards town.

Chapter Four

Voit's door swung open and a young soldier stood there with a wild look in his eyes. "Sir, they've escaped."

Why wasn't Voit surprised? He knew there was more to that Angel character than met the eye. He shouldn't have underestimated him.

"Sir. Should we send out a search party?" He wasn't twitching, but Voit knew he wanted to. He had that effect on some of the younger men.

Voit had to think about that. Should they waste their energy searching or find out just who this Angel and his partner were? It wasn't like they could really go anywhere right now and Voit wasn't going to fix their ship so they could get off the planet. Their fleet was under lock and key. No way could they leave.

"No. Not yet. I'm going to go find out what is going on with their ship. It's not like they can go far and it'll get cold soon. My guess is they headed up into the mountains. They'll have to come back eventually for supplies. Just let the town know to be on the lookout." Voit left his office and went to the ship. There had to be some clue on the damn thing. He'd left earlier because there was nothing he could do. He really should just leave his people to it but he was concerned. Usually he didn't like to micromanage, but they had to know something by now. The ship wasn't that big.

Tok was overseeing the crew set up on the ship. Two men were going through it looking for clues and their computer man was searching the coms.

"Anything yet?" Voit glanced around.

There really wasn't much to see on the ship itself. The odd thing was it appeared like it was only set up for one person—he'd noticed that the first time he'd come to the engineer's bay.

Tok was the one to answer, "Not yet. The system was locked."

"What about damage to the hull?" Voit waved behind him towards the door.

"The engineers have gone over it. It appears as if it was shot at one point. Part of the engine caught fire and caused it to crash," Tok explained patiently. "Won't be too hard to fix with the right equipment. It's a nice little ship."

"So you don't think they were sent here to spy?" Voit tapped on his lip and continued to poking around.

"Not from what you told me. I think most of what Angel said to you was the truth. I'm not sure why he picked here when he thought it to be uninhabitable. But it would be a good hideout spot." Tok shrugged. "You know that is why our ancestors came here to begin with. The Alliance wasn't looking here. It just had a big no-fly zone attached to the space."

"They're going to send someone here soon. You know it. It's a viable planet now and they think of it as theirs."

"That's why we need to petition them, Voit. If we go to them first and show them what we've done, I think they'll leave us alone." Tok threw down whatever he'd been messing with and got into Voit's personal space—almost touching his shirt.

There were others around and Tok should've known better. Voit had to be the one in charge and they both knew it. If they thought Voit was getting weak who knew what would happen. Voit's family had been the backbone of Earth from the beginning when they'd been getting things up and running again. Voit had an image to protect and it wouldn't look good if people thought he was fooling around with his second-in-command.

"What about what our parents and grandparents wanted? Does family and loyalty mean nothing to you?" Voit poked Tok in the chest. His dark purple skin flushed.

He'd gone too far and he knew it. Tok and his species had settled with them on Earth when they'd been pushed out because the rest of the Consortium had wanted to merge with the Alliance and not have to worry about it anymore. They'd said they were tired and it was time for someone else to take over. The Delphini race hadn't thought it had been the right thing to do—that one power shouldn't control the whole galaxy. They had been for merging and adding consortium members to a council with the Alliance. The Delphini were a peaceful people for the most part.

They were also a beautiful people—humanoid in every way except for their purple skin and the fact that they had no body hair at all. And Voit had explored every inch of Tok's body, but that had been when he had called him Archer and they'd been kids with nothing to lose.

Tok was one of the most loyal men he knew and he hated to see him all stiff and looking pissed off. Voit was being a jackass. Another reason they shouldn't ever be more then friends. Tok needed someone who could just be his — their ship had sailed a long time ago and they were both very different individuals now.

"Commander Reno, I am your advisor. That is what I am doing. I will follow what you wish, but I want you to think about everything. We both know the history of Earth. Do we want a repeat? The Alliance to come here and bomb us until the planet is unliveable again? Where will we go then? And if that is all — *sir* — I have work to do."

He didn't wait for Voit to dismiss him. He stormed off to the other side of the bay.

Damn it. He needed Tok, if for nothing more than to set him straight. He had a lot of thinking to do. Voit did know what Earth had been through before his people had settled there. It was the reason the Alliance was in existence to begin with. And they'd been forced off the planet because of war. Now they controlled the galaxy. Voit had no idea if they were any good at it either. Their ancestors had cut off all communications. He had been lucky to find contacts among the Alliance to begin with. Maybe it was time to talk to them now. They could have some insight to the whole thing.

Should they really team up with them? Where would that leave Earth? Would a force come and invade and take over when they knew it was habitable? The last time he'd spoken to his inside man, Patric, he and his brother, Bill, had been visiting. That had been over five years ago. They'd needed a break and had come to Earth to get away from the grind of whatever it was they did within the Alliance. Tok and his crew had met up with them on the outer ring of the solar system while they had been foraging for electronics to bring back to Earth. Patric had been very entertaining in and out of bed and he had been happy with the Alliance. Had even told Voit to give him a call sometime. Voit had checked in a couple of times, but nothing much had changed. Patric was still happy enough.

Maybe his family had it all wrong. He hated having to be in charge and figure all this shit out. Damn it. For once he wished things would be taken out of his hands and someone else would fix the problem. He stared at Tok's back for a few more minutes before turning and leaving the ship. They would report to him when they were finished and he had a call to make.

The room was dark and Angel had to let his eyes adjust. He'd left Frank on the far side of town in a house that had looked abandoned. It was starting to get cold and he had to get back before Frank froze to death. Damn this fucking planet.

Next time, idiot, think with your big head.

God he was so stupid. He should have trusted his brother to make sure Frank stayed safe, but damn it, Angel needed to think of himself sometimes and he wanted Frank more than anyone he'd ever wanted before and he was going to have him. Not the Alliance and not Vincent. No—Frank was Angel's and Angel wasn't sharing.

He'd spent so many years undercover and he was taking a fucking break. Of course, his brother probably knew that by now. He'd basically gone rogue and hadn't checked in with the Alliance in a while. He just hoped his family wasn't too worried.

Fuck, he'd screwed up big this time. Angel tiptoed through the offices, pulling out his ninja-like skills Frank had joked about. It wasn't far from the truth. Angel was good at blending in, which was why they used him in covert ops.

The building that housed the jail was the first place Angel stopped. If it was him and he was in charge of the town, he'd live in the spot where he worked — if he was a bachelor. He was taking a guess that the commander would be holed up there. He hoped he was right, because he wanted to get back to Frank. And soon.

His hunch paid off. He entered the office where he'd been questioned. He remembered a door, and when he opened it, the good commander was right there, sleeping on a smallish cot.

Angel moved to the head of the bed and got into position. He needed answers and he was worried that the commander would fight him over it. Not that he blamed the man.

He crouched down and got his hands ready to cover Voit Reno's mouth. Like a good soldier, Voit sensed his presence even in sleep. His eyes shot open and Angel slapped his hands over Voit's mouth so he wouldn't scream out.

"I need you to be very quiet and listen to what I have to say. You and I are going to help each other out. Nod if you understand."

Voit nodded.

"Good. Now — I'm going to remove my hands, but only if you promise not to call out. Do I have your word?"

Again, Voit nodded.

Angel eased his hands away.

"I should have expected you to show up." Voit sat up and turned so his back was to the wall.

"Why is that?" Angel really was curious, but he needed to get down to business.

"It's what I would have done." Voit shrugged.

He was making it hard to dislike him.

"Okay, then. Now that we have that settled let's get to business. I know you aren't Alliance and I know this—" Was he really going to tell this guy who he was? Yes, he was now the idiot who told everyone his secret identity. He was going to undercover hell. That's all there was to it. He cleared his throat. "Because I'm Commandant Angel Carter."

Voit just gave him a blank stare. Did he not know who Angel was? Or what the hierarchy of the Alliance was?

"This is supposed to mean something to me?" Voit crossed his arms over his chest and glared.

"Well, I guess not. Let me explain. I am one of the top leaders in the Alliance. I'm in charge of the undercover operations to weed out the bad seeds. My brother, my father and my father's boss are the only people over me at this time."

"Shit. You've come to take over, haven't you?" Voit stood up.

The blanket that had been covering him slipped to the floor, showing every inch of the good commander, and he was very nice to look at with dark hair covering his chest. Angel let his gaze travel lower and Voit started to get hard. He must have noticed because he picked up the blanket and wrapped it around himself.

Angel shook his head. He was really losing it. The ogling wasn't necessary and while the commander was nice, he wasn't Frank. That got him back on track.

"Take over what? I had no idea anyone was here. As far as I knew, the planet might still be toxic. I don't have the scientific researchers on speed dial and I've been a bit busy with other things." Angel moved so he could lean against the far wall and kept his eyes on Voit. He knew he looked relaxed—he was anything but and could spring to action if needed.

"Why here then? You could have gone anywhere. Now will you tell me who you're running from?"

"I don't know."

And he didn't. When he'd taken off with Frank it had been just to get him out of the situation. He knew his brother could handle things and they wouldn't need Frank for a while. Angel had figured he'd have had him back before stuff started happening.

He'd planned on taking Frank to one of the pleasure planets to relax for a bit and heal while they got to know each other. So he could see how he could really help Frank and maybe scratch the itch he'd had for the past few months while he had been working with Frank. They'd got off the planet just fine, but then someone had shot at them.

Angel had managed to get away, but he still had no idea who could be after them. Then they'd crashed and he had had other things to think of.

"How is that possible?"

"I'm undercover. I have people after me. It could be anyone."

"Will they follow you here?"

"I don't think so. But on to bigger things—why are you here and why aren't you a part of the Alliance?"

Chapter Five

Voit wondered how far he could trust Angel. He'd really underestimated the guy. He'd thought for sure he'd have to go searching for him, and after his talk with Patric he was willing to entertain a few ideas, and now—how convenient that an Alliance official was there. Voit ran a hand down his face. It was a coincidence, he knew it, but he hated it. It made everything feel...off, and Angel was a cocky bastard as it was.

He had to trust Tok's instincts and get things started so his people didn't die in something senseless he could prevent.

"When the Alliance took over the galaxy, they pushed out some of the Consortium who didn't fully agree with them being the only power. Those were my ancestors. They left and ended up here. We've been on Earth ever since and we've rebuilt it to what you see today. I—" He was going to do it—he just had to get the words out.

Think about your people – the families – and do this.

"I want to petition the Alliance to join them."

What had he just done? He wanted to take the words back, but it was too late.

"Okay, not my department, but we can get that ball rolling." Angel shrugged.

"That's it?" Voit looked at him in disbelief. All of his worry and he had got an...okay? Un-fucking-believable.

"What more is there? We need to start finding people we can trust to make sure the Alliance stays uncorrupted. As long as you don't plan on some sort of takeover..." Angel glared at him and Voit had the decency to blush. "Yeah, that's what I thought." Angel snorted, but continued. "I don't see an issue with you and your people staying here and going on like you have been. The Alliance isn't a bully—you've established this part of the galaxy as yours fair and square. It was empty and you settled on it. Done deal in my opinion. Now that we have that all situated and we aren't enemies, I'd really like a warm place for Frank and I to spend the night and I need to see if I can get my ship fixed. As well as check in—my family is going to be worried. Plus, Frank is still injured and this could can't be good for him. And maybe drugs for the pain."

Voit plopped down on the bed. That had been too easy. All his fears—they had been pointless. Tok had been right. Shit, he totally didn't want to tell him that, but there was no other choice.

"Ah, yeah, go wait in my office and I'll get you some keys. You can stay at my folks' old place for the night and we can talk more in the morning. As for the meds, we'll have to make a pit stop on the way to the house."

Angel looked him up and down before walking out of his room. Yeah, he totally wasn't going there. Voit rushed to find clothes so he could dress and get Angel settled. The morning couldn't arrive soon enough for him. He wanted to put his mind at ease and have things put together in the official channels. When he'd contacted Patric he'd said the Alliance was doing a big crackdown on corruption and some people had already been arrested.

He wondered if that had anything to do with the problems Angel had alluded to. That wasn't his issue to deal with. He had his own worries just as Angel did. Earth came first as well as the people under his command. He'd have to contact with his people in other parts of the world to let them know what was going on.

Lost in thought, he almost ran right into Angel. He was sat on the edge of Voit's desk.

"Get off my desk."

Angel just grinned at him. Voit shook his head and pushed at Angel until he moved, then rummaged in his desk to find what he was searching for.

"Where did you stash your partner?" Voit didn't even glance up.

"Other side of town in an abandoned shack."

"Oh yeah, the old Thomas homestead. Not the best place to hole up. Follow me." Voit walked out of the door and didn't turn to see if Angel followed. He wondered just who Frank was to him.

Voit had been alone a long time and Angel was a very attractive, if smug, man. He'd tap that, and Angel had to like men with the way he'd studied Voit.

Not. Going. To Happen. He might tap that, but he hadn't got where he was by thinking with his cock and he wasn't about to start now. Angel would probably be gone as soon as they got his ship fixed and Voit needed him to smooth the way with the Alliance. He had to take in the bigger picture.

It didn't take long to get to the hospital. Voit checked in at the front desk.

"Hey, Merrill, I have a guy that one of the medics tended to earlier and I need to see about getting some pain meds for him. Can you help me out?"

The nice things about living in one of the smaller communities on the planet was how everyone knew everyone else. They kept most of the colonisation that way. It was easier, but every year they were expanding.

"Do you remember which medic, sir?" Merrill didn't glance up from his paperwork.

"I think it was Dawn." Voit tapped his finger on the desk.

"I'll page her to the front."

"Thanks, Merrill."

Voit turned to see Angel checking the place out. It wasn't a big building, not like the hospital in the next town over. A lot of folks had said he should move his offices to one of the bigger cities, but he was happy where he was, and who would suspect that the whole planet was run in this little town?

He'd studied history, and the larger places were the first ones targeted. With all the department heads spread out it would make it harder to take down their infrastructure. Or at least he hoped it would. It helped him sleep better at night.

Angel had his back to the wall and was watching the door.

"Everything okay?" Voit asked.

Angel glanced over at Voit. God, they needed to hurry. The temperature was dropping and he wondered if Frank would think to start a fire—he probably wouldn't because he'd have no clue that they had no need to hide the evidence of their whereabouts any longer. They should have gone to Frank first, but the medicine was important. Neither one of them were dressed for the colder weather and Frank had nothing but what he was wearing. Angel wasn't sure if any of his clothes would fit him. He'd have to see if he could get some things from his ship after they'd settled for the night. Not like Voit had to worry about him flying off.

"Yeah, I'm good. Just want to make sure Frank is okay. The temperature seems to be dropping pretty fast. I know his wound is better, but I just want to be on the safe side."

"We'll be done in a second and we can get him before we head to the house."

He knew he was being silly. It wasn't like him, but he had no point of reference on how he should act. He was starting—fuck he didn't even want to think it—to have feelings for Frank. Somehow the criminal had wormed his way under Angel's skin. Fucking bastard. Didn't he know Angel didn't have time for this shit?

The medic from earlier came up and talked to Voit, but Angel wasn't really paying attention. He was thinking two steps ahead. He was wondering how soon they could get his ship fixed. He hated seeing the *Avenger* so torn apart. It had been his home for so many years.

Not even the pirates had dared to try to take it away. They knew better. But it was time to retire. Really retire. A pleasure planet was looking awful nice right about now. He closed his eyes. He felt safe enough in the hospital now that he knew Voit wasn't going to try to ransom him off or something worse.

He could see himself on a lounger by the pool, lying down with his shades on, listening to a book and sipping an ice-cold beer. It would be so hot that when Frank stood over him and dripped water from the pool onto his skin he'd jump…

And he really did jump because Voit put a hand on his shoulder, breaking him out of his daydream. Shit, he was getting soft. It really was time to get out of this job. Too many people could get hurt if he pulled a stunt like that on a mission.

"Hold onto that instakill there, slugger. I've got what we need, let's go." Voit slapped his back and walked out of the door.

Angel followed Voit from the hospital. He couldn't even get away from Frank in his fantasies. He was so screwed — maybe he could make that in a good way if Frank was feeling better.

If he could, he'd slap himself in the head. His dick didn't control him. He was above that. Maybe.

The shack was a bit of a walk from the hospital. Angel had picked it because it was on the edge of town and looked like it hadn't been lived in for a very long time. When they opened the door, Frank was fast asleep on the floor and shivering. Angel had no idea how he could sleep like that.

He rushed over to make sure it wasn't fever induced. If it was, they were going back to the hospital. His wound shouldn't still be affecting him this way. Was there something else wrong with him?

Frank wasn't hot to the touch and the second Angel touched him, he bolted upright and clutched at his side.

"Motherfucker!" Frank all but screamed.

"Well, I was going to ask you how you feel, but I think I got it." Angel chuckled.

"You scared me, damn it." Frank pushed Angel's hand away.

"You shouldn't have been sleeping. What if I was someone else?" Angel stood and held out a hand to help Frank up.

"Like me." Voit peeped up from behind Angel.

Angel shook his head and Frank scrambled to his feet.

"Nice going there, Voit." Angel turned to glare at the man. He crossed his arms over his chest and stood firm. He didn't like to see Frank hurt and that little stunt hadn't helped.

Voit held up his hand, but he was laughing.

"Sorry." Voit tossed something to Frank. "Here's a pain killer to help with your side. We should get headed out now so we can get the heat going in the house. It'll be cold there too." Voit turned and strode to the door.

"Come on, Frank. Time to move. Think bed and heat." Angel winked at him.

"What the fuck, man? You leave and I'm supposed to hide out and then you come back with the enemy?" Frank wasn't budging and Voit was still leaving.

"I'll explain on the way. He's going to help us, okay? In return I'm going to help him. And tonight we sleep in a real bed and have some heat instead of bunking here on the floor in the cold."

Frank didn't say anything, just followed the commander. Angel brought up the rear and closed the door. He was happy to see the last of that cabin. They'd only been in it for a couple of hours, but it left much to be desired. There were holes in the wall and rats crawling around. Angel shuddered. Not much got to him, but he hated those rodents.

As he was walking he noticed what a nice round ass Frank had. He wanted to see it without the pants. He'd been waiting for that for a few months. He'd thought Frank wanted the same thing, but now he wasn't so sure. Tonight he was going to find out.

Chapter Six

Frank was shivering harder by the time they had reached a little ranch-style house. He hadn't seen one of those except on ancient vids he'd perused at the black market. Most of his time had been spent in warehouses or apartments. He could picture himself living in a place like this—doing what, he had no idea. He wasn't trained for much of anything.

His side ached like a bitch, but he didn't want to complain too much. It had settled down until he had been scared shitless with Angel touching him. He'd been having a really vivid dream about dancing naked through flowers—with Angel. It was a silly dream, but he'd felt peaceful for the first time in...forever. He hadn't felt that content since he was a young boy sharing the day with his mom. They all each other had and he really needed to contact her soon before she freaked out. No one wanted to get in the way of Ally Morgan when she went on a rampage.

Of course, he'd never told Angel about his mom—hadn't really told Angel much in the way of anything except that he'd testify or do whatever was necessary to stay out of jail. He had some cash put away. The life of crime wasn't too glamorous, but it did tend to pay well, and no matter what happened, he wasn't giving that money up.

"All right, gentlemen, I'm going to leave you to get rest. We'll talk in the morning. There are blankets in the hall closet, the bathroom is down the hall and to your left, and there is still some food left in the fridge. My folks haven't been gone that long and it should still be good. There is wood by the fireplace and the thermostat is by the hall closet." Voit handed Angel what looked like a communicator. "If you need anything before morning, here is my com. It'll go straight to me. Good evening."

Frank was trying to process everything, but this was so different from being in a jail cell. And a fireplace? He didn't think houses had those anymore. He wondered what else might be different, but he was having trouble concentrating because Angel was moving around the room checking it out.

"What are you doing?" Frank really was curious.

"Just making sure everything is on the up and up." He was turning things over and running his hands along the walls—knocking every now and again. He made Frank tired just watching him.

"I'm going to take one of these and go to bed." Frank shook the bottle Voit had tossed his way at the shack and turned to look for the kitchen.

The space wasn't very big so it wasn't hard to find. The water still ran and there were cups in the cupboard. He tossed back just one pill. He didn't want to feel groggy and one would take the edge off enough so that he could have a deep sleep instead of the restless tossing and turning.

He wondered how many bedrooms there were. Angel had followed him into the kitchen. He must have been satisfied with the living room area. Frank held the glass to his mouth and paused. Angel was giving him an odd look, one that he wasn't sure about—was that lust in his eyes? Frank licked his lips and Angel groaned. Frank put the glass down before he dropped it. This wasn't really unexpected. The sexual tension between them had been through the roof for a long time.

Frank used to get pissed when Vincent would make some cavalier remark about taking Angel's ass. God, he'd never wanted to hurt someone so bad as he had in that moment.

"Angel?" He had to clear his throat.

His cock was hard and he wanted to kiss Angel. Fuck, he wanted more than a kiss, he wanted inside Angel's ass. Hell, he'd even take Angel's dick up *his* ass. He really didn't care.

"I want to fuck you, Frank." Angel hadn't moved. "Tell me 'no' now, or this is happening."

Frank didn't answer. He pushed away from the sink and got into Angel's face. He had to look up a bit and stand on his tiptoes but he was so close he could taste Angel. He brushed their lips together and whispered against Angel's mouth, "Then fuck me."

Angel grabbed his head and Frank forgot about any pain. Angel kissed him like he was the last sweet on the planet, nipping at his lips and licking his way inside Frank's mouth. Frank wrapped his arms around Angel to bring him closer. He winced a bit at the pressure, but there was no way he was going to stop this. He wanted Angel. They were both panting when Angel pulled back.

"We need a bed."

Frank nodded at Angel. That would make things a bit easier. He didn't want the pain stopping him from feeling Angel. He took the hand Angel had offered and they stumbled through the house until they found a room. Frank didn't wait for Angel. He peeled his clothes off as he headed for the bed so he could lay down, not caring where they landed. The pill was kicking in and the pain was a dull throb. By the time Angel's dick was in his hole he wanted that to be the only thing he was feeling.

Frank sprawled on the bed — on his hands and knees with his butt in the air. Angel tapped it.

"Not this way. You're going to ride me."

He gulped. He was used to the slam-bams where they just got off — riding would be more…intimate. But he wanted that so bad with Angel. He nodded and moved to the head of the bed, giving Angel room to lie down. His gaze wondered over Angel's body. He was perfect, right down to the angel tattoo on his shoulder. Frank would have to explore that later. He wished he'd watched Angel strip off his clothes, but that would be a next time thing too.

Angel opened his arms and Frank positioned himself over Angel's body so he could reach his lips. They kissed lazily for a while like they had all the time in the world. Well, they did have all night. Frank was beginning to warm up, but he still shivered as Angel ran his hands down his body and squeezed his cheeks. Frank spread his legs so they were far enough apart that Angel could play with his ass.

Damn, they didn't have any lube. Not like Frank had been thinking of sex when he'd been carried off the last planet they'd been on. They didn't have any gear either and he didn't think Angel was that prepared. The cold liquid coated his hole took him by surprise.

Frank lifted up and looked down at Angel. He waved a bottle of oil at him. When had he…? Frank shook his head and continued to kiss Angel. He moved on to his throat, scraping his teeth over the tendons and soothing it with his tongue. He nipped at Angel's chin before he squatted over Angel.

"Angel, do something," Frank murmured against Angel's chest.

"Patience."

"We can do that next time. Get in my ass."

Angel rewarded him by sliding his finger in Frank's hole and rubbing on his gland. A second finger soon followed and Frank rocked back and forth.

"Frank…"

He pushed at Angel's fingers and got into position. He had Angel's cock in one hand and held out the other hand for some oil. Angel put some in his palm and Frank coated Angel's dick, taking long slow strokes.

"God, you're going to feel so good inside me."

Angel's hips bucked and Frank eased Angel's shaft into his hole. It burned, but it was so good. It had been a long time for him and he couldn't remember it ever feeling this intense. He wasn't going to last too long. Damn it. He wanted it to go on all night. He paused when he had Angel's balls resting against him. Frank was fully seated with his hands on Angel's chest to steady himself. The pain from his ribs was a thing of the past. All of his nerve endings were on fire—the hairs on his arms were even standing up. Every inch of his body belonged to Angel at that moment.

"Frank, move."

"Wasn't it you who said 'patience'?" Frank chuckled and clenched his ass.

Angel moaned and thrust upward. "Do"—he gasped—"as I say—not...oh shit...not...so good...fuck—as I do." Angel gripped his hips.

Frank leaned over to kiss Angel, almost letting Angel's cock slip out of his hole.

Angel whimpered and sat up. He had one hand on the bed and one around Frank's body, holding him steady. Frank moved up and down on Angel's dick, each stroke tapping his prostate. Angel finally wrapped him tight in his arms, helping him shift.

"Angel...close..."

"Too soon. Too soon," Angel chanted.

Frank agreed, but he wasn't going to be able to stop himself.

Angel gripped his hips tight so he couldn't budge and put his head on Frank's chest. They were both breathing really hard and Frank could tell Angel was as close as he was. But stayed still.

"Angel...please...let me...oh, God. So...good. So good. Angel, Angel..." Frank flexed his ass, but Angel still held him in his grip.

"Minute. Hold on." Angel flipped them over and held Frank's legs open wide. He took Frank's dick in his hands and stroked it with each thrust into his ass.

There it was, that feeling. It raced up his spine and he shouted out. He heard Angel scream his name before he collapsed on top of him.

They panted and Frank petted Angel's sweaty back.

"Let me..." Angel tried to roll off him, but Frank wouldn't let him. It felt too good. "Your wound," Angel began.

"Can't feel it. Shh." Frank had his eyes closed and just wanted to savour the moment.

"M'kay." Angel licked Frank's lips.

Frank angled his head down and brushed his mouth against Angel's. Nothing too deep, just an 'I'm here, thank you, let's go again' kind of smooch.

Frank wanted to get his lips wrapped around Angel's dick and planned on doing that happening a bit later. Maybe after a shower. They could do with some downtime after all they'd been through, and Frank was going to take advantage of the night if nothing else. No other first time had been this explosive. Of course his other times had mostly been made up of one-night stands. It didn't feel that way with Angel.

"Stop thinking so hard. Let's shower," Angel had said the words, but didn't leave his spot on Frank's chest.

He chuckled, pushed Angel and rolled off the bed, holding out a hand. They'd managed to find a bedroom that had bathing chambers in it. Frank tugged Angel until they were inside the room. He turned on the water and let Angel get in first. His ass was sticky. Whatever Angel had used didn't feel as great now that the sex was over.

Frank turned around so the spray hit his butt.

"Sore?" Angel fingered Frank's hole.

"No, sticky. What was that stuff?"

Angel chuckled. "Some kind of oil. It just looked wet."

"I didn't even see you grab it." There was no soap in the shower. Frank should have thought of that, but Angel had really blown his mind. Maybe next time it'd be his shaft. He could picture Angel's lips spread around it. He ran a thumb over Angel's mouth, forgetting what he'd been thinking. Oh, soap.

Frank got out of the shower and searched the bathroom until he found a bar.

"I grabbed it while you were taking your clothes off." Angel's voice came from behind the curtain.

He joined him back in the shower and began lathering up Angel's body. He could touch Angel for days and never get bored. He wanted to lick every inch of him, but he'd have to rinse the soap off first. Frank knelt and focused on Angel's length. He used his hands to suds it up, making sure not to miss an inch. Once it was clean and rinsed off, he slid Angel's dick into his mouth and hummed.

"Frank!"

Frank grinned around the cock filling his mouth. Angel tasted clean and was growing with each suck. He pulsed in Frank's mouth. Angel reached for him and pulled Frank off his cock.

"Too much, Frank." Angel kissed him and tugged both of their shafts in his hand. He stroked them together.

Frank rose up on his toes. It was so good. "Angel—"

He shouldn't be hard again this soon, but he was and he was going to shoot off faster this time.

"I'm there, Frank. Come with me."

That was all it took. He had to hold on to the wall or he would have fallen down.

"Angel—"

He didn't know what he had been going to say, but Angel stopped him with a sweet kiss.

"Let's go to bed."

Frank agreed. He was too tired to do much of anything else. They dried off and snuggled into bed. Another new experience for Frank.

Chapter Seven

An explosion woke Angel. He shot out of the bed so fast he fell on his ass. He had the presence of mind to grab Frank and drag him down with him to the floor. Frank grunted on impact.

"What the fuck?" Frank rolled over to glare at him.

"Didn't you hear —?"

He was interrupted when another blast shook the house.

"Well, I heard that." Frank crawled to where his clothes littered the floor and began to dress.

"What are you doing?"

"Looks pretty obvious, doesn't it? I sure as fuck don't want to get caught naked." Frank cocked an eyebrow.

"Shit." Angel scrambled for his pants and struggled into them.

"We should see if Voit needs help," he said as he buttoned his pants.

"Hell no, we should find cover."

"They could be here because of us."

"How do you figure, Angel?" Frank covered his chest.

Angel almost groaned but managed to control himself. It was a close call.

I need my head in the game, not worrying about Frank putting his fuckin' clothes on.

"I have enemies that could have followed me. Not to mention if someone found out you were going to go all tattletale on them and they could want you dead. The safest place for us is with Voit and his men."

"Fine, but you and I both know the first place they're going to hit is any government building."

"All right, let's head to the engineers bay. The *Avenger* is in there and we can see how much damage is done in case we need to vacate the premises. It's not like we can help evacuate everyone, but maybe they're trying to get ships in the air. If this isn't about us, I want to know who would be hitting a supposedly empty planet."

"It's always about money and power. I figured you'd know that by now." Frank walked out of the room.

Angel was stunned for a moment but he hurried up and got into his boots so he could follow Frank's tight ass out of the door and...he needed to stop thinking about Frank's ass. He was getting hard in spite of the urgency of their situation. Adrenaline did stupid things to a person.

"Not everything has to be about power." Angel looked around as he caught up with Frank.

"Of course it does. Isn't that why you're one of the heads of the Alliance?" Frank glanced over at him.

Another blast hit the ground and Angel watched the light reflect off Frank's face.

God, Frank's gorgeous.

"No." Angel cleared his throat. "No — that's called family tradition and wanting to see justice. Why do you think I'm undercover and not sitting at some desk? Hell, half the people *in* the Alliance think I'm dead and we've kept it that way for years."

"Not everyone is you, Angel. Most do-gooders don't last as long as you have." Frank slung an arm over his shoulder.

They'd reached the bay where the *Avenger* was stashed. It was total chaos. Angel spotted the guard from the other night — Tok he thought his name was. He walked over to where the guard was giving orders.

"Hey, can we help? Where's Voit?" Angel looked around but didn't see the commander in the mess.

"Ahh, the Alliance Saviour. I heard you'd finally talked Voit into applying for entrance to the Alliance." Tok handed a box off to someone and turned to face Angel.

"He asked." Angel shrugged.

It really wasn't that big of a deal. At least not to him.

"He's over at the Command Centre, just on the edge of town. One of the rundown shacks."

"Hiding in plain sight. Very nice. Thanks."

Tok nodded at him. Angel turned and left. They were no use in the bay and would only get in the way. Frank fell into step beside him. The explosions had calmed down. Thank goodness. It looked like most of the people had stayed in their homes. The activity seemed to have been around the ships.

* * * *

They finally reached the location where Tok said Voit would be and Angel knocked on the shed — the only one that had any light leaking through the windows.

"Come in," Voit called from inside.

Angel pushed the door open to find Voit pulling his hair.

"Can we help?" Angel walked closer.

"What the fuck did you bring down on my planet, Angel?" Voit stood and glared at him.

"I've no idea what you're talking about."

"Somebody knows you're here. They want you something fierce."

"Well, let's give them what they want."

"What?" Frank yelled.

Angel had been formulating a plan in case this was about him. It wasn't the best plan, but it might buy them some time.

"Calm down. Let me explain."

Frank crossed his arms over his chest and didn't back down, but he let Angel talk.

He's so fucking hot like that, all puffed up, has me wishing for a bed. Damn it. Not the time. Not the time.

Maybe if he kept telling himself that, he'd believe it.

"Well?" Frank grinned like he knew what Angel was thinking.

Bastard.

"Voit, do you have any ships you don't mind getting rid of?"

"A couple, sure." Voit nodded.

"Okay, I propose you tell them you're sending me off planet in my ship."

"Ang—" Frank walked closer.

"Let me finish, Frank. Is the *Avenger* anywhere near flight worthy?"

"I think we can launch it." Voit seemed more curious now.

Good — it had to work for all of their sakes.

"How about warp?" Angel knew the ship had issues or it wouldn't have crashed, he just hoped it wasn't the warp drive.

"I'll have to ask Tok."

"Okay, ask them to give you some time to get me on the ship. We can check while they wait. We'll programme the *Avenger* towards an outer galaxy. After we do that, we'll take your ship and attempt to hide its signature, but not too hard. We want them to think we pulled a switch. Then I'll make a few calls. If I don't find out what I need to, I'll contact my brother."

Frank had eased his stance a bit as Angel had talked. Like Angel would sacrifice himself after finding Frank. He might be crazy, but he wasn't stupid.

Frank wasn't happy, but at least Angel wasn't going to go out in a blaze of glory. He knew the type of guy Angel was. He might have said it was all about the power, but in his heart he knew that wasn't the case. Frank wasn't good enough for Angel. He needed to turn himself in, testify if it was needed, then disappear. Sure it would hurt, but it would be worth it for Angel. This was the first time he'd regretted his life of crime. For him it had been about love and money. The love had faded, but the money hadn't. His mom and sister were set up and would never want for anything. Growing up, that hadn't been the case. But that was still his excuse for his life of crime.

Frank moved out of the way and watched Voit and Angel work out the plan. There was really nothing he could do.

"Give me half an hour to get him airborne and he's yours," Voit said over the com.

"You've got ten minutes," said a gravelly voice coming from the tiny computer on the console.

"I need more time. The ship is in questionable shape." Voit sounded frustrated.

"Give him a different one." The person on the other end didn't sound like he was in the bargaining mood.

Voit must have thought the same thing. "Ten minutes it is."

Angel reached over and pushed the off button.

"That'll be all we'll need. It'll be okay. I've come out of worse situations."

Was that a grin on Angel's face? It was. Frank shook his head. Leave it to him to be excited at something that could backfire and get them all killed. Frank walked over to Angel and could almost feel him vibrating.

"You're enjoying yourself, aren't you?" Frank whispered in his ear.

It was worth it to see his lover shiver.

"Yeah, kinda. Weird, huh?" Angel gave him a sheepish look.

"Nope. You're in your element. Doing that good thing you do. That's why—" Frank paused.

He wasn't...he didn't—shit—when had that happened? He fuckin' loved Angel.

Angel gave him a curious glance but didn't say anything. Frank was so screwed. No wonder he was trying to go all noble and leave. Well, fuck that. Angel was his now and he wasn't giving him back.

They left the shack and headed towards the loading bay where the engineers kept the ships.

"We really should leave so this doesn't come back on the planet." Frank changed the subject. No way was he telling Angel he loved him. Not yet and not in front of anyone else. When he told him, he wanted to be able to get him naked and enjoy his body.

"It'll still come back to them, and even if we leave they won't believe Voit. Our best bet is to get the Alliance involved. I'm not sure where their nearest warship is." Angel tapped his chin.

"We aren't even part of the Alliance yet. Will they help?" Voit interrupted.

Frank had almost forgotten Voit was there. That's what he got for daydreaming about Angel—naked and begging for Frank to fuck him.

"Because I told you, you're part of it now even if nothing formal has been written up. We protect our own." Angel's tone brooked no argument.

"If—" Frank swallowed. "If they come, will they be taking me with them when they leave?"

He'd almost let himself forget that his life really wasn't his own anymore.

"Not happening. We'll figure something out." Angel squeezed his hand.

They arrived at the *Avenger* and it looked in bad shape, charred and dented. He could see where the fire had done its damage. Frank had no idea how they were going to get it into space. The internal systems were probably even worse off than the outside of the craft.

Even though the bombs had stopped, people were still running around. Three or four of them were crawling all over Angel's ship.

"So you're just going to send your ship out? And what about when this is all over?" Frank waved his hand around the bay.

"I have a tracking device. We'll go get her when this is finished." Angel winked at him and headed towards the guard.

He'd said 'we'. That made Frank feel a bit better, like maybe Angel might have feelings for him. But they'd have to talk about that later. He felt so useless standing there, but he had no idea what to do. He was used to the boss giving orders and he just obeyed them. No questions asked. Time was running out. He did know that.

"Fuck," Angel shouted.

Frank ran to where he was standing. "What is it?"

"The warp drive is giving us fits," Tok said. "We might have to change up the plan a bit. Get the *Avenger* out there then shoot the Earth ship into hyper drive and make them follow it." He had his hands on his hips, staring at the ship.

"We're running out of time so let's do this." Voit rubbed his hands together.

It looked like he was enjoying the situation as much as Angel. They were both insane.

"Okay," Angel said. "I need a com station so I can contact my dad. I think he'll be the most helpful right now. He can locate a war ship. When it gets here it can patrol the area in case they come back. Hopefully it isn't too far out. If it is, we need a contingency plan to keep your people safe, Voit. I also really need to find out who these people are." Angel was very decisive.

Frank knew it wasn't the time or place, but he was so turned on. Fuck, if his cock didn't get hard. Angel was bent over a counter and Frank wanted to take him right there. Not caring if people were watching. They needed to get a handle on the situation and he was thinking about sex. He wanted to talk to Angel, but who knew when they'd be alone again.

"Frank. Hey, Frank, you ready?"

Him and his stupid daydreaming. He nodded and followed Angel out of the ship bay—again.

"I need to do something, Angel. I can't just—"

"Goddamn it," Tok shouted, interrupting Frank.

"What?" Angel sounded concerned.

"We have more problems. We need someone to manually fly this out of the atmosphere. It has warp capability, but the technology isn't as advanced as on the *Avenger* and we're out of time."

"I'll do it," Frank volunteered, speaking out before he'd even really thought about what he'd said.

"No you fucking won't." Angel stood with his hands clenched by his sides, his eyes flashing fire.

"No time to argue. You have to contact the Alliance, it's not like I can help with that. I'm an extra set of hands." Now that he'd made the decision he felt better.

"Time's running out," Tok reminded them.

Angel strode over to him and took Frank's face in his hands, giving him a hard kiss on the lips.

"Don't die." Angel nodded and turned, leaving Frank to climb into the craft.

Shit, this had been a bad idea, but he'd rather it be him than Angel. He was no hero. Never really had been, but he had no regrets, if this kept Angel alive.

"Here goes nothing," he said under his breath.

He watched the *Avenger* move out of the bay and shoot into the sky. He wasn't far behind.

Chapter Eight

Angel shook.

Stupid fucking hero.

Wasn't that supposed to be his job? Angel ran a hand down his face.

"He'll be fine." Voit clasped him on the shoulder.

Angel gave him a weak smile. "Show me the coms. The sooner we get this taken care of the better."

He could still hear the whoosh of the ship leaving the atmosphere. Angel didn't want to leave the bay and didn't know how long he'd been standing there. He had no idea how Frank was or if he was even going to be safe. It didn't help that they had no idea who was gunning for him. He hated not knowing. Now he knew how his family felt when he went silent for months at a time.

Angel walked with Voit to the coms station set up in the shack on the outskirts of town, and Voit showed him a board with tons of buttons. He hadn't seen anything like it in over a decade. It was old. He just hoped it would patch him through. Hell, the last time he'd seen something this antiquated it was back in the training camps.

He pushed in his father's personal frequency and prayed to all above it would work.

"Commandant Carter."

Thank fuck.

"Dad?"

"Angel? Son, is that you?"

"Yes, sir." No matter how old he got, his dad would always be sir. It had been ingrained in his mind from birth.

"What's wrong?"

"Why does—"

"Cut the bullshit, son," his dad interrupted.

"All right then. I'm on Earth." Angel figured he'd pull out the big guns first. Give his dad a bit of a shock for calling bullshit on him.

"What the—?"

"Yes, you heard that right. Earth and…" He looked over at Voit, who nodded his consent. "It's populated."

There was a brief pause and he wondered if he'd lost the connection.

"Stop pulling my leg, Angel," his father warned.

"I'm not. They want to sign on with the Alliance, but we can talk about that later."

"We can? I don't—"

Angel wasn't sure how long they could stay connected and he had to get this bit out. "Dad, listen, someone is after me and Frank—fuck, Frank is out there and—"

"You aren't making any sense. Who is Frank?"

He didn't blame his father for being puzzled. "I love him, Dad." Well, he shouldn't have blurted that out. He hadn't even told Frank yet.

"Start from the beginning."

"I was with Alphonse and I, well, I helped him out, no matter what he might tell you. He was supposed to take Frank, an informant—"

"A criminal."

Angel could picture his dad's lips thinning out on the words and his nostrils flaring, like he was right there in front of Angel showing his disapproval.

"An *informant* in to help his case. Frank was shot so I got him out of there. The ship was attacked by pirates on the way and I finally ended up in Earth's atmosphere. I was crashing. We were picked up at the crash site and greeted by Commander Voit Reno, and he requested to petition the Alliance for admittance." Angel left out the part about the jail cell. His dad didn't need to know everything. "The planet was attacked and I want to request—"

"Hold on. I'm getting a message. It's from your brother. It seems he's had feeler out and someone spotted your ship moments ago and boarded. It was found ransacked and bloodied. I don't like this, Angel. Are you being coerced?"

"No. Shit. That was Frank's blood. I told you he was shot. The wound got bad and started bleeding when it shouldn't have. Everything is on the up and up down here," Angel assured his father.

"Well, you're in luck because your brother will be heading your way shortly with the *Reward*."

"That was fast. We just launched the ship a few minutes ago. How is that possible?"

"Your brother was worried about you. He's been searching for you since you took off. You're just lucky he sent someone so far to look for you."

"The *Reward*? Is that an Alliance vessel?"

"It is now. Alphonse's partner—"

It was his turn to shout, "Wait—what?" Angel's brother had a partner?

"You aren't the only one on the move, boy. I expect you here as soon as this mess is cleared up."

"Yes, sir." Communication was cut his dad could hear the sir.

"So…" Voit looked at him expectantly.

"If my brother is coming we can get your petition out of the way. I have to tell you, though, the Alliance is going to want help on your part." Angel crossed his arms and leaned against the console. He figured this wouldn't go that well, but he wanted to be open and honest with Voit.

"Help with what? It's not like we have much and what we do have is so out of date it's pathetic." Voit had sounded suspicious.

"With people. I told you the Alliance has been cleaning house—well, I told you or Frank, it's been so crazy lately I'm losing my mind. I could have told you both." Angel waved that off because he couldn't even think of Frank right now.

"Okay, so how does that affect us?"

"I like what I see and tend to trust my instincts. You, Tok, the others, we need reliable people. We could set up an outpost here, rotate people in and out. Send you people in return. If there is anyone who'd like to move to fill in some vacated spots, I'd be willing to entertain that as well. So would my brother."

"I want to go."

Angel hadn't seen Tok walk in. The man was worse than he was for sneaking up on people.

"Tok…what…" Voit seemed shocked.

"You don't need me here, Voit."

If Angel wasn't mistaken, Tok looked sad.

"But I do."

Angel wanted to leave, the moment seemed too personal to have someone watching, but Tok had come in, wanted to join up with the Alliance and Angel had to see that through. They really did need people they could trust.

"No. You don't." Tok shook his head.

He spoke up to hopefully ease some of the tension. "I gotta say, Tok would be greatly appreciated. I've seen how loyal he is to you."

"We've known each other a long time and you can't take all my warriors. Who will protect Earth?" Voit glared at him.

"That's what the Alliance is for, but they wouldn't want all of them. Just a bit of fresh blood. Too much corruption going on there now. Your people are used to a different way of life. If Tok would agree to come with me, or go with my brother, we can set up an exchange programme. But he can talk to you about that later. He knows more than I do — my brother, that is. I've been away for a long time."

The crackle of the coms made Angel stop talking.

"Mayday, mayday. Angel, fuck…this thing…on? I've no weapons and they are about to board. Shit. The hatch is opening…they have me locked in…I can't get…Goddamn it. Shit."

"Stand up. Wait — you aren't Angel."

"I know you, don't I? Who…why are you — "

Crack.

The line went dead. What the fuck? No. This couldn't be happening. Frank had just left orbit. Angel slammed his fist into the console.

Frank opened his eyes. He really didn't want to, but the pounding was getting worse. The last thing he remembered was reaching out to Earth — to Angel, then the boarding party. He had no idea if his transmission had even gone through. They hadn't been too pleased that he wasn't Angel, but he happened to be very happy that Angel wasn't on board that ship. Fuck. He'd recognised one of the men who'd boarded the ship. He really needed to stop passing out on strange ships.

"Well, well, well, if it isn't Vincent's right-hand man. What were you doing with Mr Angel?"

And there it was – the face and voice finally clicked into place. Chuck Steel, Vincent's silent partner. The one helping with the deal that had gone bad thanks, in part, to Frank. But why did he want Angel? No one had expected Angel to be an agent. He was too efficient as a hitman.

Frank cleared his throat. "Does it really matter?" He shrugged, playing nonchalant.

"Yes, Frank, it does." Chuck had sounded like he was speaking to a child and it irritated Frank, but he didn't say anything. "Angel isn't who we thought. Seems he's Alliance. He fucked up the deal. I know it and I want him dead." Chuck caressed the laser gun in his arms with a gleeful look in his eyes.

If Frank thought Vincent was nuts he *knew* Chuck was certifiable. That was why he was the silent partner. Vincent never let him out of his cage, so to speak. At least not that Frank knew of. What did this mean about Vincent if Chuck was on the loose?

"You talkin' about the same Angel I know?" Frank would try to play it off. It might be his only chance to survive to see Angel again. He didn't know jack shit and needed all the help he could get. He hated not being informed.

"Yeah, I am. We managed to break in to a communication before we were cut off. So why were you with him?" Chuck was pressing him now.

Not too hard, but he was starting to crowd Frank's space — almost getting into his face. Frank wondered how much Chuck really knew.

"We were sent out, by Vincent." Frank glanced around him as he moved so his back was to the wall — he really had nowhere else to go, he was stuck there and he was becoming uneasy with the way Chuck was glaring at him. The ship wasn't much to look at with its dull grey walls. He was in some sort of holding cell. Another thing he would really like to avoid in the future.

"Bullshit." Chuck crouched down by Frank and slapped the wall by his head before moving back to the door.

"When was the last time you spoke to Vincent, Chuck?" Frank was just happy the tremor hadn't shown up in his voice. Chuck could really lose it at any minute.

"A while," Chuck hedged.

"And?" Now Frank pressed him.

"I got word he was dead." Chuck peered down at his feet and shifted from side to side like he was searching for some sort of comfort. He tapped his fingers against the end of the laser.

Frank hadn't been aware that there was a rumour regarding Vincent's demise. He hadn't asked because too much had been going on. He remembered being shot, then nothing else until he woke up on Angel's ship, then again in the cell. He wondered if he'd still have to testify or if this made his deal null and void. It would suck if it was off the table because he had no idea what it would mean for his future. Frank gulped.

First he had to make it out alive. That's what he'd focus on, not Angel and not what their future could hold. There'd be time for that when this fiasco was over and done with.

No one had expected Chuck. At least he hadn't. Frank figured the Alliance would have to root him out in order to prosecute him once Frank gave over his information.

"Who'd you hear that from?" Frank laid his head back on the wall hoping to ease some of the pounding. He had to stall, keep Chuck talking.

"I have my sources." Chuck sniffed and ran a hand under his nose.

Frank tried to remember the plan if they got caught. Vincent always had something up his sleeve. Yes — go to ground. Re-group. He had to play this just right — get Chuck on his side so he wasn't so defensive and maybe he'd put that damn laser down.

"He's not, you know." Frank moved so he could look at Chuck.

"Again, I call bullshit."

The laser pointed his way. He really didn't want to get shot again.

"He's in hiding." Frank held up his hands, trying to reassure Chuck.

"Vincent would have contacted me."

Now Chuck was pouting. What was up with that? He'd never had this much contact with Chuck and his up and down moods. How had Vincent dealt with him?

"I don't think he had time. They were comin' in hot and we scattered. I went with Angel."

"Why am I hearing he's Alliance then? And where is your partner — Lorenz? Why didn't you leave with him instead of Angel?"

Frank stood. It took a bit to get his balance, his fucking head hurt. "I told ya, to ground. Everyone is. No way were we going together, everyone knows we're partners, it would look suspicious. What I want to know is, why the fuck are you out here with guns blazin'?"

"I'll ask the fucking questions, Frank." Chuck pushed him back down.

Frank growled, "Asshole."

"Now, if you're on the up and up, why did you flee the planet? Why not just invite me down to hide out with you?"

"You were firing on us and making demands. It was easier to get your attention this way, plus I had no way of knowing it was you. You never identified yourself. If you had commed us and told us who you were things might have gone a bit different. As it was, I needed to get you away before someone noticed an idiot firing on a planet and alerted the Alliance. Then where would we be, Chuck?"

"What's it matter. The place is supposed to be empty anyway." Chuck shrugged and went back to tap, tap, tapping on the weapon, hugging it close to him like a security blanket.

"Well, it's not. It's full of people loyal to Vincent and you fucked up royally. He's gonna be pissed." Frank stood back up and smirked.

This is kinda fun – if I forget about the gun and the fact that the lunatic wants to kill Angel.

"Fuck." Chuck began to pace and mutter things Frank couldn't understand.

"How long have I been out?"

"Day and a half. You're such a wimp. My man didn't hit you that hard." Chuck stopped long enough to point and laugh.

Angel was going to be furious, but at least he wasn't dead—yet.

"Fuck you, Chuck. I've already been shot and I'm having issues."

No wonder his head hurt so badly. He just wanted to go back to bed. Preferably in Angel's arms. He was lucky he hadn't slipped into a coma or something. Fucking head wounds. And the bastard had let him sleep it off. Even Frank knew you weren't supposed to do that.

"Now what? I can't have Vincent upset with me. I just can't." Chuck tugged on his hair, his eyes wild and unfocused.

"We call Angel."

God, he hoped Chuck went along with him.

"No."

Shit. It was like dealing with a kid.

"What do you mean, no, Chuck?" Frank towered over Chuck and glared down at him.

"I don't trust him. He's not one of us, you know?" Chuck slapped Frank's chest like they were old friends sharing a joke. "Plus, Vincent had a thing for the bastard. I still want him dead, like an accident, you know—can't let Vincent know I done it, right?" Chuck grinned. "You won't tell." Chuck pointed the laser at him again as if that sealed the deal.

Frank sighed. It was going to be one of *those* days. Could it get any nuttier?

"You don't have to worry," Frank assured Chuck.

"I don't?" Chuck tilted his head, curious.

"Nope. Angel's taken."

Chuck snorted. "By who?" Like it couldn't happen— Angel being taken. Boy, did Chuck have a surprise in store.

Frank would use what he could to get Chuck to stop thinking of Angel as the enemy—even if in reality Angel was going to be Chuck's worst nightmare.

"Me." Frank grinned.

Chapter Nine

"It's almost been two days, Voit."

"Voit, just got a com there's a ship in orbit and it's hailing us." Tok peeked into the room.

They were back in Voit's office and all Angel had managed to do was wear a path into the carpet with his constant pacing. It should have been him on that ship. He could have contacted the Alliance en route.

"Patch them through here." Voit's voice brought him back to the situation at hand.

Progress was being had on the *Avenger*—, at least that was something. They'd pulled it back down after Frank had left. If there was an Alliance ship out there, the one who'd informed his brother, nobody had seen it—they must have left orbit after contacting Alphonse. And it wasn't like he could go after Frank. They could pinpoint where the distress call had come from, maybe, but he knew Frank wouldn't be there. He could be anywhere by now, or, heaven forbid, dead. But he couldn't think that way, not if he wanted to keep his sanity.

"This is the *Reward* requesting permission to land."

The *Reward*? That was—hot damn, his brother had finally showed up. Now maybe they could get somewhere—the technology on his ship had to be better than what they had on the planet. He really needed to see about getting Earth into this century.

"Permission granted." Voit turned towards him. "Good news, yes?"

"Yes." Angel stood and grinned for the first time in days. Thing were looking up and maybe Frank would be alive—he had to have hope.

"Great. I was getting tired of mopey Angel." Voit snickered.

Angel heard Tok in the other room laughing as well.

"Bad idea to poke at me, Tok—Alliance training starts soon and I might have a *bit* of pull." He was used to being the one people feared, but he didn't have to play a role here with these people, he was just Angel. It was kind of nice—but he still had a darker side to pull out when he needed it.

That shut Tok up, but not Voit. If anything he laughed harder. Angel shook his head and wondered, not for the first time, what was up with those two.

"Let's go greet the ship." Angel rubbed his hands in anticipation.

The sooner they informed his brother of the situation the sooner they'd take action, and Angel wouldn't feel so useless.

They walked over to an old docking bay and waited. The hatch opened and Angel saw his brother, Alphonse, striding towards him. He opened his arms for a hug, but got a punch in the face instead.

"What the fuck, Alphonse?" Angel rubbed at his jaw and got up off the ground. His brother knew how to throw a punch. That shit hurt.

A man held Alphonse back. He was pretty sure that it was the guy from the warehouse back on that pleasure planet and he wondered if he was his brother's partner. Whoever he was, Angel wanted him to let Al go so he he'd be able to hit him back—a fight was always a good stress reliever and he'd been stressed for a while now.

"You couldn't contact me? No, I had to get a report of your ship, abandoned no less, by *Earth*, with blood all over the place."

Angel shrugged. "I called Dad."

"Motherfucker."

"Yeah, he is." Angel grinned and pulled his brother to him. "I missed you." Angel released Alphonse.

"Why did you run, Angel?"

"I...ah...wasn't thinking straight?" And wasn't that the truth.

"I hate to break up the family love here, but I want a tour. Damn if I'm not on Earth. James, in case you forgot." James held out his hand for Angel, but Angel pulled him close for a hug too—after all, James was family now according to his dad.

"Don't hurt my brother or I'll kill you." Angel wasn't above threatening even if James was family.

James just laughed. He might be chuckling now, but he wouldn't be when Angel's foot was so far up his ass James would taste it. He took being a big brother seriously. And what was it with people laughing at him. Usually they trembled in fear—even when he was in nice mode.

"Tour later. We need to find out what's going on," Alphonse insisted.

"We can go to my office," Voit piped up.

"Oh, sorry. Alphonse, James, this is Commander Voit Reno. He's in charge here."

"Oh good, I have tons of questions…ah…later." James looked like a kid in a candy store.

Angel shook his head. There really wasn't much difference on Earth to some of the other planets. He didn't see the big deal.

"Voit, this is my brother Alphonse and his partner James," Angel finished the introductions.

He fell in step with his brother on the walk back.

"What's going on?"

"I'm not sure, Al. Someone is after me, but I don't know why."

"Where's Frank?"

"He…" Shit this was hard. He wanted Frank back and he had no idea if he was dead or alive, damn it.

"Ang?" Alphonse grasped his shoulder.

"Sorry…yeah…he led the attackers off and they captured him."

"What is he to you, Ang? Give me the straight answer, not one you'd give Dad."

"He's…fuck, Al…he's everything. And yeah — Dad already knows too."

"Damn."

"I know. Now he's out there…alone. There haven't been any ransom demands or anything. I know they want me, but no way. And Frank could be dead because it was him in that ship and not me." Angel wiped a hand down his face.

"We'll find him," Alphonse assured him.

"We have to." Angel was at his wits' end.

"So, why Earth?"

"It was supposed to be deserted." Angel shrugged. "I wanted a place to hide out and who would come looking here?" He waved a hand around the town. "Well, besides you obviously, since you sent a ship out this way."

"We sent ships *everywhere* and lucked out. I had no idea where you'd go to ground, you have a way of hiding that I admire, but yeah, you can see how excited Jimmy is to be here. He's always wanted to see Earth."

"Where is your ship, you know, the one that spotted the *Avenger*? We didn't see it and I looked."

"Once we found out where the ship was we sent them back. I planned on checking it out myself anyway and then Dad let me know you were actually on planet and not still out there somewhere — captured or dead."

"The timing was…unreal."

"I'm going with lucky." Alphonse winked.

They reached the office and Tok was waiting for them. "I just got the strangest call."

"What?" Voit asked.

"It was Frank. He wouldn't let me say anything, kept cutting me off."

"So, he's fine?" Angel had to grab the wall so he didn't fall over.

Frank was alive. Angel closed his eyes and took a deep breath, trying to get himself under control.

"He is. He's bringing some guy named Chuck Steel with him."

"Fuckin' shit. Goddamn motherfucker." Angel kicked the door.

"I take it you know him?" Tok's tone was dry.

"Yes. We suspected he was working with Vincent but never got confirmation. One of the reasons I tapped Frank—" He had to stop because his brother was laughing so hard. Angel glared at him and continued. "He has information on this guy. He's bad news. A very loose cannon and we're going to have to play this carefully or someone *will* die."

The reports on Chuck were so outlandish that Angel didn't know what was true and what wasn't, but he hadn't had time to get the information from Frank. They'd been concentrating on Vincent at the time.

"This could be a trap, Angel. Did you ever think of that? There are now two top officials—" James paused when Alphonse interrupted him.

"Three on the way." Alphonse held up his fingers.

"What?" Angel twirled to face him.

"Dad's coming."

"Fuck, no." Angel sat down, hard.

This was unbelievable. His dad never came to them. They were always ordered to report to him.

"Fuck, yes," Alphonse assured him, sounding just as stunned as Angel was about the situation.

"He told me to come to him."

"He wasn't taking any chances." Alphonse shrugged.

"As I was saying, three officials of the Alliance. Wasn't that Vincent's ultimate plan? To take over? Now three of you are in one place and Frank is out there…" James trailed off.

"No." Angel would never believe that. Not of Frank. Not anymore. Maybe when they'd first met and he'd been feeling him out to see if he would turn. But not now after they'd spent time together. Frank wasn't just a thug.

"Let me finish—" James tried to say more.

"No. Frank isn't dirty."

"Are you a hundred per cent sure of that, Angel?" James pushed.

"Yes." He wasn't going to question Frank's loyalty to him.

They hadn't seen his face when Frank had left on that ship to save lives. They wouldn't know him like he did and they needed to get over the fact that he'd worked for Vincent. That wasn't who Frank was anymore.

"Willing to risk your life? Your dad's? How about your brother's life or the fact that a known criminal is out there?"

"Alphonse, pull your boy off," Angel growled.

"He's got a point, Ang."

"Not you too." Angel couldn't even look at them. He was disgusted with the lot. Of course, they didn't know Frank like he did, but it didn't give them call to question his trust. They should take the fact that he had faith in Frank and deal with it.

"If you want my input, Frank is on the up and up," Tok broke in. "I saw the way he looked at you, Angel. You can't fake that." Tok turned to Voit, then glanced quickly away.

"Okay, enough of that. How long do we have?" Angel just wanted Frank back and this shit wasn't helping.

"Frank didn't get far from the point where the SOS call came in from. Maybe a few hours." Tok assured him.

"We need to hide the *Reward*. We also need to get into positions for when they land. I want to be visible, but the rest of you need to spread out and hide. The less people Chuck sees at first contact the better." Angel was thinking of all the things he needed to do to make it easier to get Frank away from Chuck.

"Do you think it'll matter?" Alphonse crinkled his brow in concentration.

"You've heard the stories about Chuck. I know you have. He's a crazy fuck, but he pays attention. We still don't know why he's after me. We take any precautions we can. Now let's go get Frank back."

Frank paced his cabin and hoped things went down like they should. Anything could go wrong. Chuck had let him make a call and he'd talked to Tok but hadn't said much. Frank didn't want Chuck to be anything but calm.

"We're approaching Earth." Chuck leaned against his door.

"Good."

"Will Vincent be there?" Chuck actually licked his lips.

Frank didn't even want to think about Chuck pervin' on Vincent. It gave him the creeps.

"I don't know. He didn't give me a time to meet up with him. Just told me to head to Earth, he had people there."

"And you're sure about this Angel?"

"I'm fucking him, Chuck. I've got it under control." God, he hoped Angel played along. Too many unknown factors for his liking. Someone was going to get hurt, he just knew it.

"You'd better or he's dead." Chuck sneered.

"Stop threatening me, Chuck."

"You may be Vincent's right-hand man, but I'm—" Chuck paused and had a confused look on his face.

"Yeah, just what are you to Vincent? You can't be his lover. Not with all the boys he has parading in and out of his bedroom." It wasn't the best idea to antagonise the crazy man, but he'd had about enough of this ship and the company.

"You'll shut the fuck up right now and stop talking about Vinny that way." Chuck stood up taller and looked more confident now. The mood swings were making Frank a bit sick. He couldn't keep up with his reactions.

"Vinny is it? Does he know you call him that?" Frank arched an eyebrow.

Chuck flinched. That's what Frank thought. Vincent had always been a hard man and no one took liberties, not even with his name, unless he wanted something from you and you really, really didn't want Vincent to want anything from you. Well, at least he didn't, Frank wasn't too sure about Chuck.

"You just keep Angel on a leash. If he looks at me wrong, he's dead. And Vincent better be there or someone needs to have some news on his whereabouts." Chuck turned and stomped away like a child who'd had a toy taken away and was going to tattle.

Frank really wished he could talk to Angel before they landed. At least they were expecting them and wouldn't shoot them out of the sky as they landed. He'd grab what he could get at this point.

They must not have gone far after Frank had been knocked out. Before he knew it they were walking towards the hatch. Frank took a deep breath—he could do this. The only person he saw was Angel. Frank closed his eyes and released the air he'd been holding in his lungs. He glanced at Chuck and the man was caressing the damn laser again and giving Angel the evil eye. Shit, he hoped Chuck could keep it in check for just a bit longer. Frank had a bad feeling deep in his gut that something was going to go wrong and he wanted to throw up, but he got control of himself. He searched around and thought he saw a couple of other people. It could be a trick of the light too, or wishful thinking on his part.

He didn't give Chuck a chance to stop him, because if anything went wrong he had to touch Angel one last time. He rushed to Angel and pulled him into his arms before he began to really panic. He hadn't thought he'd ever be in this position again and it felt good, really, really good. He didn't want it to be the last time. It couldn't be. This had to work.

"Play along," he whispered in Angel's ear before kissing him on the cheek. He felt the slight nod.

"Where's Vincent?" Chuck demanded.

"Dead."

Frank turned around and shoved Angel behind him. Who the fuck was that and why were they opening their big fucking mouth? This was going to be very, very bad.

"What's he talkin' about, Frank?" Chuck said through clenched teeth.

Frank glanced between the moron and Chuck, trying to think of a way to fix this.

"He's wrong, Chuck. Who ya gonna believe? Me" — Frank lifted his chin — "or a stranger?" He nodded to the left where Big Mouth was standing.

Fuck, fuck, fuck. Of all the —

Chuck had his laser out and he was shaking. Frank knew he was going to get shot again. Shit.

"I'm just going to shoot you all. How's that sound to you, Frank? Did you lie to me? Is Angel really Alliance scum?" Chuck's voice was getting louder and his eyes had that glazed, deranged light in them.

Things were spiralling out of control. Fast.

"If you put the laser down I'll take you to the coms. I'll break silence and contact Vincent."

"But—"

Frank glared at the idiot who wouldn't shut up.

"You do that, Frank, but if you're lying, pretty boy here is dead." Chuck waved the laser towards Angel.

Damn it. No, just no, I can't let Angel be hurt.

"No worries, Frank." Angel stroked a hand down his back.

He knew it was to comfort him, but all it made Frank want was more and to be alone with Angel — away from all the nuttiness.

"I know, babe. I told Chuck things were under control, right, Chuck?" Frank didn't look away from Angel — not yet. Frank patted Angel on the check. "You coming, Chuck?" He hated turning his back on the man, but he had to show Chuck he wasn't concerned.

He was shaking inside. It was going to fall apart. He braced himself for the blast of the laser, knowing Chuck really could break down at any second. He was walking a fine line and he usually didn't speak crazy. Frank took a quick peek behind him.

"I'm coming." Chuck sniffed but didn't lower his weapon — his aim solely on Angel.

Frank couldn't even say anything without Chuck hearing. He had to get all of them out of this with no injuries. Well, except Big Mouth — he could do with a flesh wound. Not that he was bitter or anything. Stupid fuck.

"Someone needs to take care of Big Mouth," Frank muttered loud enough for all to hear. It would serve the idiot right, it really would.

"Alphonse will take care of things," Angel assured him.

Alphonse? Wasn't that Angel's brother? Maybe things weren't as bad as he'd thought. He hadn't seen any ships in orbit when they'd landed, but it looked like the cavalry had arrived. If things didn't work out he was shooting Big Mouth himself. Fucker.

Someone slammed into his back. He heard the laser go off and everything began to happen in slow motion. Angel fell beside him and there was shouting, but Frank only had eyes for Angel. His lover wasn't even twitching. Frank shook Angel's shoulder and there it was—movement. Frank breathed a sigh of relief. Thank fucking God. He closed his eyes.

"Frank. You okay, man?" Angel stroked his shoulder.

"Maybe." Frank didn't want him to stop touching him.

"Were you hit?"

"Nope. You?"

"No. Don't know how neither of us were. My dumb ass brother jumped the gun." Angel had raised his voice at the end.

"Not my fault, pretty boy." Alphonse snickered.

"Anyone else hit?" Angel shouted.

A chorus of 'nope'—all good—circled around him. He opened his eyes to see Angel staring at him.

"Hi," Angel whispered.

"Hi," Frank whispered back.

"Do that to me again and I'll shoot you myself." Angel swooped down and kissed him.

Chapter Ten

Angel was livid. Stupid James had opened his big fat mouth and had almost ruined everything. He couldn't get enough of Frank's lips. He was there and not dead. At least Frank had followed directions.

Someone kicked him in the back.

"Umph."

Angel turned to see his brother grinning at him. He scowled back.

"Get a room, pretty boy."

"Stop calling me that. And you" — Angel stood and pointed a finger at James — "what the fuck were you thinking telling that maniac Vincent was dead?"

James had the decency to look sheepish. "Hey, no one said anything about keeping it a secret and it *is* true."

While he was berating James, Frank had stood up and was advancing on James.

"You fucker. If you don't know, don't say. Simple as that. Keep your trap shut!"

"Ang, pull your guy off before I get violent."

"Alphonse, I think Frank has a right to be pissed. James almost got us shot."

"That's right. *Almost.* If you weren't so busy playing sucky face you would have realised it was James who took loony bins out." Alphonse pointed to the ground where a very angry-looking Chuck struggled in his bonds.

Angel got down on his haunches. "So, you and Vincent? I think we need to talk."

"I ain't sayin' shit." Chuck spat in Angel's direction, but he managed to dodge it.

"He doesn't have to, Angel. We both know that," Frank piped up.

"You shut up, Frank." Chuck fought harder against the restraints and it appeared as if he was trying to wiggle closer to Frank.

"Yeah, and why is that, Frank?" Angel didn't look away from Chuck. He wanted to see his reaction.

"I knew Chuck was Vincent's silent partner. What I didn't know was Chuck here had a thing for my ex-boss."

"You can't prove anything, Frank." Chuck smirked, but he'd stopped fighting.

Tok and Voit managed to get him standing.

"See, that's where you're wrong, Chuck. I have access to all of Vincent's dealings and he liked to keep extensive notes." Frank glanced over at Angel. "Blackmail," he said in a loud whisper.

"Not on me he didn't." Chuck had almost sounded smug.

"Oh, he didn't have blackmail on you, no, he knew you'd come running at any hint he'd give it up for you. But, I have bank transactions as well as vid-cam conversations. Why do you think I made a deal? I wanted out."

Chuck shrunk in on himself before Angel's eyes. He wasn't...anything. His eyes had gone dead like no one was home. What Frank had said must have got through to him.

Angel glanced over at his brother. He was frowning at something.

"What is it?" God, he hoped it wasn't more bad news.

"Dad's here."

And his hopes were dashed. "Fuck."

"Yeah," Alphonse agreed.

"I'm taking Frank out of here."

"You're going to have to talk to him eventually." Alphonse didn't have to look so happy about that.

"Not yet. Later." Angel tugged Frank away.

"Did he just say your—" Frank pointed behind him.

"He did. Dear old Dad is about to land."

Angel kept them walking. He touched any part of Frank he could reach, just to prove to himself that Frank was really there and alive.

He wanted viral proof—the naked kind where they rejoiced in being alive. And hot...and sweaty, maybe even a bit sticky.

"Fuck." Frank's eyes widened.

"My thoughts exactly." Angel nodded and smiled.

Yep, a good hot fuck then some slow lovemaking and maybe another round for good measure.

"You...Dad...I can't...we just..."

It was so cute hearing Frank stutter. Angel ran a hand down Frank's backside and pinched it. Naked would be a good thing—but they should get inside first. No need to show off the goods.

"A bit soon to meet the family, I know, but let me help you forget about it for a little bit."

Frank still looked confused. Angel took him to the house where they'd had sex the first time — the place he'd been staying while Frank had been gone too. It felt like a lifetime ago and he needed to touch Frank. Wanted Frank inside him. He'd never had the need before. Usually he was the guy who said no ass play, but this was Frank, not that he'd never had someone fuck him, but that would have been when he'd first started exploring.

Angel paused at the door and pushed Frank against it, pressing their lips together. "I want you to make love to me, Frank."

Frank's gasp was enough for Angel to slip his tongue inside and take the kiss deeper. He was getting hard and needed to be out of his pants. He moved away and pulled Frank from the door, but Frank didn't budge. Angel jerked back — he hadn't been expecting the resistance.

"Did you just say — ?" Frank all but whispered.

"Having troubles there, Frank?" Angel grinned and cupped Frank's cock through his pants.

"I wouldn't be if you and your brother would stop trying to shock me." Frank was panting now.

Angel could tell he was getting just as excited about the prospect of hot 'I'm so alive' sex.

Angel grabbed Frank's shirt and brought him closer. "Not trying to shock you, just letting you know what I want. Now, you coming?" Angel winked.

"Not yet — but soon I'm sure."

Angel threw back his head and laughed. He had to wipe at his eyes. Not at all what he'd been expecting, but that was a good thing. Frank kept him on his toes.

"Now that" — Angel pointed at Frank — "that sounds like something I'd say."

Angel opened the door to the house and pushed Frank inside, shutting and locking the door behind them.

"I thought I was going to lose you, Angel." Frank was back to whispering, his voice hoarse, and tears pooled in his eyes.

Angel couldn't have that. There would be time to reflect later. Right now? It was time to prove that they hadn't lost each other.

"At least you followed directions." Angel pulled Frank's shirt off.

"Huh?" Frank returned the favour.

"Remember—don't die." Angel kissed Frank on the forehead. He brushed his hands over Frank's nipples and caressed his stomach.

That had been one of the most important orders he'd ever given and he'd never been as thankful as he was right now that it had been followed to the letter.

"Oh, right—yeah, close call, huh?" Frank nodded. He touched and stroked Angel's skin as well. They couldn't get enough of each other and they weren't even completely undressed yet.

"Never again," Angel breathed. The words had been almost silent, but Frank must have heard him because he stopped moving.

"What?" Angel was confused—they were getting naked, right? And he'd meant it—never. It couldn't happen again or Angel might not make it. Frank would understand. He had to.

"It's your job. How can you say that?" Frank tilted his head to one side, studying Angel.

"Oh..." Angel waved that off. "I'm retiring." He went back to trying to get Frank out of his pants. He should have had him take his boots off first, but he wasn't thinking straight. It took him a second to realise Frank still hadn't budged. Getting naked was supposed to be a joint effort.

"Angel, you can't just quit." Frank put both hands on one of Angel's shoulders to stop him.

"The hell I can't. I'm done, I put in my time," Angel assured him and hoped they'd get back to naked time.

"They still need you," Frank almost pleaded with him.

"Bull." He was too old to keep up the undercover stuff and he might have been exposed—it was time to hang his hat up and retire. He didn't understand why Frank was so concerned. It would be better for both of them if he quit.

"Weren't you talking about corruption?" Frank tried again, but Angel wasn't having it. At least not yet.

"Can't we talk about this later?" Angel palmed Frank's cock through his briefs with one hand, still tugging at his own pants to get them off. Frank was no help at all. Damn it. They needed skin. The sooner the better.

"Later. Yes. I won't forget, Angel," Frank warned.

"Whatever. Get naked." Angel licked his lips in anticipation.

Frank shivered and toed off his boots. This was what Angel was talking about. Frank stood in front of him—bare. Angel tugged at his pants again, tossing them aside, his boots and socks—everything, until they stood there just looking at each other.

Frank was nervous. It wasn't like he hadn't topped before, but he'd never thought Angel would let him. He didn't seem like the kind of guy who gave up any kind of control easily and here he was waiting for Frank to take charge. And he wouldn't forget. He couldn't—not about the Alliance. They needed men like Angel—but he would think about that later. Right now there was too much naked Angel to explore and he wanted him spread out.

"Bedroom, Angel."

Angel nodded and Frank watched his ass as he walked. Frank gulped. It was a big step for him, taking a man who was all about control and making him want what Frank had to give.

Angel crawled onto the bed and opened his legs, his cock hard against his stomach. Not too long ago, in that very bed, it had been him all laid out for Angel. He was going to take advantage of the situation.

"I love you, Angel."

Frank hadn't been expecting to say that, but he hadn't been able to hold it in, the moment was too big. They had been getting to know each other for months and Frank was a better person because of Angel, he believed that with all his heart. Before he'd met the Alliance agent he would have never volunteered himself for a mission that might have killed him to save others. It was all about him, but no more. If he hadn't met Angel, he might be dead now, thanks to his former life—but that was the past and it would stay there as far as he was concerned.

"I love you too, Frank. Now come fuck me." Angel smiled and took his cock in his hand, stroking it slow and steady.

No way—that was his dick tonight and he'd show Angel just how much he loved him. Later they could worry about the future. For now, he was going to live in the moment. The outside world faded away. It was just the two of them in that bedroom. Frank smacked Angel's fingers.

"Mine," he growled.

"Yours," Angel agreed and stretched his arms above his head, holding onto the headboard.

Frank nodded then moved to the bottom of the bed. He hadn't thought it was possible to be this hard, but the picture of Angel spread out just for him was mind boggling. He kissed the top of Angel's foot and licked his ankle, working his way up to Angel's thighs. He gave a little nip to each one as he continued his path up Angel's body, exploring every inch. His hair was so light Frank almost couldn't see it. Frank nudged aside Angel's balls, he'd get to them in a minute. First he nuzzled into the juncture of Angel's thigh, scraping his teeth on the sensitive skin. He gave the other side the same attention before sucking Angel's balls into his mouth. They were salty and musky. Frank hummed in approval of the way Angel tasted. Angel was thrusting against the air, but Frank wasn't ready for his cock, not yet. He still wanted to explore.

"Frank. Frank. Please."

He ignored him, for now. He had another place he wanted to taste. He licked Angel's perineum and pushed his nose into Angel's ass crack, taking a deep breath and inhaling his scent. It was everything Angel—down to his very essence—and Frank was going to take that in. He nuzzled around Angel's hole. Angel had gone stiff above him, not even twitching. Frank began to fuck Angel with his tongue. The sounds coming out of Angel were almost enough to make him come right then and there. He spread Angel's cheeks farther apart and spat on his thumb before easing it into Angel's body. It was tight and Frank went slow, wiggling his digit around until he found Angel's prostate. He rubbed it and watched Angel light up. He added his other thumb, alternating the ins and outs. He used his tongue to keep everything wet.

They needed lube and again they were without it. Angel must have been reading his mind because something shook in his peripheral vision. It was the same oil they'd used before. That would do, but the next time they had sex, Frank was going to have the right lube.

Angel tugged at his arms. Frank reluctantly left his position and let Angel guide him on top. Angel roughly took Frank's mouth and moaned. Angel was licking and biting at Frank's lip, like he couldn't get enough.

"God, I taste so good on you. Fuck me, Frank. You're driving me crazy."

Frank hummed against Angel's lips, not sure if he was done tasting and teasing. But staring into his lover's eyes he knew it was time. Frank felt around for the oil and, he coated his cock and Angel's hole. He wanted it this way—staring into Angel's eyes as he fell apart in his arms. Frank took his dick and eased it into Angel's ass an inch at a time. Angel was so tight it almost hurt, but not enough to stop. He paused when he was fully seated, giving Angel a second to adjust before he eased back out, his hips thrusting at a leisurely speed. This was about making love, not a hard fuck.

"I love you, Angel," Frank said again.

Angel took Frank's face in his hands and gazed into his eyes. The moment was so intimate it almost wasn't real.

"Love you too, Frank." Angel wrapped his legs around Frank's hips. Not urging him on, taking it slow.

It might have started out as a quick fuck, but not now. No — it became about making love — every touch, every caress showing Angel how much he loved him. How happy he was to be alive and in Angel's arms.

Their orgasms sneaked up — at least his did. He was looking at Angel when the tingle in his spine alerted him to the fact he was about to come. Angel squeezed down on him and moaned as heated liquid hit Frank's stomach. He thrust a couple more times and came inside Angel. He was sensitive, but Angel kept tightening his ass so Frank wouldn't slip out.

Frank couldn't move. He really didn't want to. Not ever. The world could stay away and he and Angel could never leave their bubble of happiness.

Someone pounded at the door. Somehow, Frank had known it wouldn't last.

Chapter Eleven

"Open the door, Angel. I know you're in there."

Damn it, his father really knew how to spoil the moment. And it had been a wonderful moment. More than he'd hoped for when he'd dragged Frank across the town. It was supposed to be fuck, then make love, but he wasn't complaining.

"Your dad?" Frank rolled off him, he put his arm across his eyes.

Angel already missed the heat of Frank's body. He didn't want to move, but if he didn't get up his dad would be barging in, and as much as he loved him, he really didn't want his dad to see him and Frank naked.

"Hold on!" Angel shouted towards the door. Then to Frank, "It is and if I don't go talk to him, he'll come in here."

The afterglow was completely gone. He was even going to try to go for some cuddling. Maybe next time. He sighed. He thought Alphonse would have had his back and given them a bit more time — wasn't that what brothers were for? Damn it.

Frank nodded and got off the bed. He was looking for something. Angel figured it was his clothes, but they'd left them...by the door. Shit. Just want he wanted, to walk out there as his dad barged in. Angel closed his eyes.

"We should get this over with. Find out what we're going to do." Frank seemed resigned.

"Not yet we don't. He can give us a day." Angel took Frank's hand and squeezed it, not letting it go, like it was his lifeline.

"Angel, he isn't only your dad, he's your boss. I'm sure he needs to make sure you're all right." Frank pulled Angel in close and kissed his cheek before he tugged his hand away.

"That might be the case, but you can stay here. I'll go—"

"And hide? I don't think so. I can't avoid him forever. I'm a known criminal and he probably has questions. Shit, you deserve better." Frank sat on the end of the bed with his head hanging down, holding it in his hands.

"I deserve you, Frank, and that's all there is to it. You had a deal in place. You'll testify and then be free to do whatever."

There was more banging on the door, but Angel ignored it. He couldn't have Frank thinking that he wasn't good enough. He was more than Angel deserved and he wasn't letting him go—father or no father.

"You know he's going to tell you I'm not good enough and he'd be right."

"Fuck that. You saved my life and who knows how many others." Angel was still a bit ticked about that too.

Frank might have never come back to him. Angel tackled him onto the bed, his dad forgotten for the moment.

"What—" Frank looked towards the bedroom door.

Angel ignored him and kissed his cheek, then his chin. He ran his hands down Frank's face, trying to memorise it by feel. He could have missed out on this because Frank had had to play hero. He wouldn't have that again. They were going to settle down somewhere and—just be. No more spy shit and no more worrying about getting shot or worse, dead.

"Angel Erik Carter you will come out here at once." His dad's voice was closer. He must have got through the front door. At least Angel had remembered to lock it or his dad might have come in earlier—not a good thing.

Without looking away from Frank, he answered his father, "If you don't want to see us naked in bed together you'd better leave. I'll come find you—later." Angel stroked a finger along Frank's chin and over his lips—he still wasn't done touching his lover.

"Angel," Frank's whisper had a sharp edge to it.

"You aren't the only one who almost lost someone, Frank. You went off to play hero and I had to stay here and hear that distress call. Do you know what it did to me? It was like having my heart ripped from my chest and all I could do was watch it being stomped on. Knowing you could be dead—I was out of my mind. Everything else can wait. Usually it's me going off and doing what needs to be done. I've seen the other side and it fucked my shit up. No more, I tell you." Angel shook his head.

Angel didn't think it was possible, but he was getting hard again. He rutted against Frank's leg.

"Your father will *not* be happy if you quit. Who says you have to do undercover stuff or something dangerous?" Frank ran his hands through Angel's hair.

He closed his eyes and enjoyed the strokes. Frank was almost petting him like a cat. He was still hard — but it wasn't as pressing as the comfort Frank was giving him.

"Listen to the boy," his dad interrupted.

Shit, was his dad standing at the door? Angel glanced over his shoulder but didn't see him. Thank fuck.

"Commandant Carter, go away." Angel had raised his voice.

"We need to talk, Ang." His father had sounded tired.

Angel didn't think he'd ever heard that tone of voice from his dad.

"He's right, Angel. You do. We can pick this up later." Frank gave him a hard kiss and pushed Angel off him.

"Everyone is against me. All right, we can let the inside world in for a bit, but not for long. Dad, we'll meet you in —"

He was going to say Voit's office when clothes flew into the room. Angel should've been embarrassed but he wasn't. It was his old man's fault for coming in when he wasn't wanted. This conversation could have waited.

"I'll be in the kitchen." His voice faded away.

Frank was laughing as he stood and grabbed his pants. Angel smacked his butt.

"Hey!" Frank rubbed at his ass but continued getting dressed.

It was a shame really, seeing that body in clothes. Frank should be forced to walk around everywhere naked so Angel could ogle him. Okay, maybe not everywhere. Frank's body was for his eyes only. Shit, he was getting hard again and he really didn't want to face his dad with a boner.

They were finally dressed and heading into the kitchen when voices reached him. Great, it looked like a big old family reunion. If he wasn't mistaken that was Alphonse and James talking to his dad. He sighed. It wasn't going to go over well when he told them he was finished with the Alliance, but he was prepared to do it. The time had come for him to get out of the family business—even if Frank thought he should stay. He was getting too old for this shit and he wanted to end up not dead at the end of the day because something got fucked up.

Frank took his hand so that they showed a united front as they entered the lion's den. All three of them turned to look as they paused in the doorway.

"Good. Let's get started. It's been a long-ass day. I still have to get back to headquarters with the prisoner along with the witness." Robert had his hands folded on the table as if he was preparing for a fight.

And he was going to get one. He didn't need to use that tone of voice when he talked about Frank It wouldn't hurt him to use Frank's name either.

"The witness has a name, Dad—it's Frank. He isn't going with you." Angel leaned against the counter, Frank stood beside him—tense. He hated his father in that moment for putting his lover through this. Angel knew Frank worried about the future. He'd all but said he didn't think he belonged with Angel, but that was total and utter bullshit.

"We need to get the ball rolling on this, son."

"He's right, Ang." Alphonse seemed sorry that he'd spoken up, especially when Angel glared at him.

"Angel…he is right." Frank had spoken so softly that he almost hadn't heard him.

Angel turned around to glare at Frank.

"No. He isn't. I can bring you when—"

Frank interrupted him.

Damn it, this was all wrong. Every bit of it. Frank should stay with him so he could protect him. Who knew how many people would go after him once they found out he was going to testify?

"I'm going with him. It's the right thing to do." Frank crossed his arms over his chest.

Angel knew that look. He wasn't going to win this argument, especially with his dad and brother on Frank's side.

"See." Robert waved a hand at Frank.

"I see nothing, Dad. Frank did a real brave thing. He deserves to be rewarded for that, not taken in like some…like—"

"A common criminal?" Frank finished for him. "That's what I am, Angel. This doesn't change my past. I need to clear that up before we can really be together. In your heart you know that." Frank put his hand on Angel's chest.

Angel covered it with his own.

"I don't like it. You'll need protection." Angel was shaking his head.

"I'll be in the Alliance's hands," Frank assured him.

"But I can't help you when I've retired." Angel wasn't above pleading. Not in this instance.

"What?" His father stood.

"Fuck no. Are you out of your mind?" Alphonse yelled, pounding his hand on the table.

Frank smiled at him and winked. Fucker. He'd let himself forget they had an audience. One that would *not* be happy with his news.

Angel turned back to the table. "I'm done with the Alliance. I've put in my time undercover. That's been blown, if Chuck can be believed. Everyone knows me as Mr Angel. Once word gets out I'm really Alliance things might get dicey. With Frank testifying, even more so. We need to get away from the Alliance. The best way to do that is if I quit."

"You don't have to quit," James finally joined the conversation.

Frank was happy someone had spoken up about quitting, even if it was that loud mouth that could have got them killed. He might have to forgive him now, damn it. It wouldn't be right for Angel to leave the Alliance. It wasn't just a job—it was his family.

"How's that, James?" Angel raised an eyebrow.

He was so fucking cocky and thought he knew everything, but he didn't. Frank knew deep down that he'd have to leave. He didn't want to, but he had to if he was really going to change his life around.

"Do what Alphonse is doing." James pointed to his lover.

"And just what is it Alphonse is doing?" Angel was glaring now.

"That's right, you don't know. I'm going to have a travelling office on the *Reward*. We could probably set the same up for you on the *Avenger*, but we might have to expand it somehow so you can conduct meetings if you have to. There is too much corruption going on and we need to be on top of it more. What better way than going to these outposts and checking in on things. You and Frank would be more of a moving target and it would be nice to have two of us out there looking for some good men to fill in some spots that have been vacated recently. Things need restructuring and that's all there is to it. Help me, Ang." Alphonse didn't look away from his brother.

"I do know of someone I want to fill one of those spots. Archer Tok. He needs some Alliance training, but he'd be ready in a matter of months. Maybe he should be the one—" Angel was trying to wiggle out of it and Frank figured it was probably because of him and he wouldn't have it.

"Stop, Angel, just stop and listen to your brother. It's a good idea." Frank tapped his fingers on Angel's chest.

"What about you? Do you want to spend all your time on a ship?" Angel gripped his hand hard.

"Right now I just want to get my past settled. After that, I don't have any plans. Well, I take that back. I need to call my mom and sister before they freak, then I'm good to go wherever you are. Don't be so stubborn."

It wouldn't be a sacrifice to follow Angel around. He'd just have to find something he could do to help. He was trained as a right-hand man, after all. Only this time it could be for a good organisation instead of for a crime boss. It couldn't be all that different.

"I like this boy." Robert nodded.

"His name is Frank. Say it with me, Dad." Angel smirked.

Frank reached over and slapped his head.

"Show some respect. He's your father *and* your boss."

"Yep, I might even like him better than you." Robert winked at him.

"We've never been formally introduced, sir. I'm Frank Morgan." He held out his hand.

"Robert Carter, and my other son, Alphonse Carter, and his partner, James Rodrick."

Frank shook hands all around and let the tension finally leave his body. He could do this. More so, he wanted to.

"I still don't like the fact that we'd be in the line of fire. I want to laze around a pleasure planet and enjoy life. I hardly know what that feels like." Angel shrugged.

"So take a vacation like a normal person while we refit the *Avenger*. Problem solved." Alphonse seemed to have an answer for everything.

"Frank still isn't going with Dad," Angel insisted.

"Angel—"

"No, Frank. I'll take you."

"Why don't you both come with me? We'll have to tow the *Avenger* in anyway. It isn't up to the travel." Robert was still standing but edging his way out of the room.

"What ship did you bring?" Angel frowned at his dad.

"The flagship—the *Allora*."

Angel sighed. "All right. Tok will be joining us and maybe a couple others who want to explore. I'll need to talk to Voit first."

"I already have a list, Ang. Got it while you were...ah...busy." Alphonse smirked.

"We'll leave you now." James took Alphonse and led him away.

They were finally alone.

"This is good, Angel. We both know it."

"I still don't know, Frank. But we have time. The trial won't happen right away and we can take that vacation. As for the Alliance—"

"What's there to think about? It's more than a job, it's your family."

"You have no idea."

"I probably don't, at least not yet, but just think of all the stuff we have to find out about each other."

"Yeah, like a sister and your mom?"

"Hey, I have a mom. Most people do." Frank laughed.

"You know what I mean."

"I do. And you can meet them. Soon. They'll be happy I'm away from Vincent and will love you for that alone." Frank pulled Angel closer and leaned against the counter. He spread his legs a bit so Angel could stand in the cradle of his thighs.

He wanted more moments like this and if things went his way they'd have them.

"How about we stop by whatever planet they're on."

"It'll be out of our way."

"So."

"If your dad doesn't mind, sure. It'll probably make up for not calling. Maybe."

Now Angel laughed.

"Right. There will be much yelling, I'm sure."

Frank smiled. The moment was perfect. Finally things were going his way and he wouldn't change a thing. Not even how he'd got to where he was because if he did that, he might not have met Angel and he was beginning to see Angel was the best thing to ever have happened to him.

He had a future and he wasn't going to ruin it. Today was going to be the start of the rest of his life. He closed his eyes and kissed Angel. Yep—complete.

Epilogue

"I'm happy you waited a few months before you left for the Alliance." Voit looked over at Tok.

They were having a beer in the local cantina. A goodbye. They'd been together for years and it hurt to think he wouldn't have Tok around. But it was a good thing. Tok needed to explore and see there was better for him out there. Voit would never see him as more than a friend. It saddened him, really. Tok was a great man and he could wish he had feelings for him all he wanted but it wasn't happening.

"I wanted to get a few things settled first with my dad. Who knows when I'll be back. It's a big galaxy out there."

"Well, you'd better come back. Don't be a stranger." Voit slapped him on the back.

"I won't. They'll be assigning me to the *Allora* for my training. I'll be working with Commandant Carter."

"Angel did say something about that. A good thing in my mind. I think they said that was the flagship of the Alliance. It's pretty big. When it was here it didn't leave orbit and the Commandant had to shuttle down."

"Yeah." Tok looked over at him and took a sip of his beer. He set it down. "You could ask me to stay."

There it was, what Voit had been dreading.

"No, I can't." He shook his head then took a sip of his beer.

"You could and you know I wouldn't leave you." Tok laid a hand on Voit's arm.

"You're meant for bigger things, Archer Tok. I'm not part of your future, but I'll always be here in your past. Don't be afraid to come back, but know…that you need to expand your horizons. You're my friend. The best I'll ever have, but we aren't supposed to be a couple."

Tok removed his hand and sighed. "I thought you might say that. I won't say it doesn't hurt, Voit, but you're right, if I stay here I'll always want what I can't have. Out there — who knows." Tok shrugged.

"Whatever happens, don't settle. That's all I ask."

"You really have no say in the matter anymore, Voit. That might sound rude, but it's true."

"I'll always have a say, Tok. I'm your friend first and foremost. Don't you forget it because if someone hurts you out there I'll find them and put the hurt down."

Tok grinned like Voit knew he would. His teeth were so very white in his dark purple face. Tok was a big man and could take care of himself, but it was the principle of the matter. He still loved Tok, just not in the way he needed to. He would miss that smile, though. It reminded him of when they were younger and getting into trouble.

"I leave in the morning. A shuttle is coming to get me and two of the other men. They are dropping off an Alliance officer too. He's going to help you scout out a few things and find a good place for an outpost."

"I know all this, Tok. What are you avoiding?"

"Saying goodbye. Earth has been my only home. I know nothing of my homeland or how things will be once I get on the *Allora*. I'm fuckin' purple, Voit. I think people will notice."

"So what if you are. There are other species out there. Who knows what you'll find. Did Angel or Frank seem put off? Or Angel's family? No, they didn't. All Angel saw was a loyal man. Nothing else matters."

"You're right, but I'm scared, okay, and I'm man enough to admit it."

"I'd be worried if you weren't nervous, Tok."

"Could you—just once—call me Archer? We might not see each other for a long time, Voit."

It had become a habit for him after they'd tried being intimate. It helped him build up a wall that Tok couldn't climb.

"Sure, Arch...anything you want. Ah..." Voit looked over at Tok. "Well, within reason." Voit laughed.

Tok gave him a sad grin and tilted his beer bottle at Voit before taking another sip.

"I'm packed and ready to go. Dad is settled."

"Don't worry, I'll check in on him. So...you're nervous, what about excited?"

"Yeah, a little. Angel said that he and Frank would be there when I reached the ship so that'll be nice. At least I'll know someone."

"Good. Good." Voit was running out of things to say.

He took another drink and looked around. The place was deserted. They'd had a big party earlier for the guys leaving—sending them off in a big way. It was the least they could do. Next they'd get ready for the Alliance invasion. He still wondered about his ancestors and why they'd fled all those years ago, but that was something they'd never written about in the history books. He'd always be left to wonder. And it wasn't a bad thing. From what he'd seen of the Alliance it was trying its best to be a force of good even through the corruption.

He wondered what the agent assigned to the planet would look like. But that would be enough of that, for tonight anyway. He was here with Tok.

"I should get to bed. The shuttle will be here early and we have a long way to go tomorrow." Tok stood and gave him a tight hug.

"I do love you, Arch. Just not the way you deserve. Find yourself out there for me, okay?" Voit hugged him back just as tight.

Tok gave him a nod and left the building.

Voit stared after him for a long time, lost in thought before giving a deep sigh and finishing off his now warm beer.

He should go too, but he really didn't want to. He hated the fact that he couldn't ask Tok to stay, but he wasn't selfish. No matter how bad he wanted to be. How did one go about forgetting the best friend he'd ever had? He didn't know, but he hoped Tok had a better time at it. That's all he could really do, wish him the best. Tok was dying a bit each day here on Earth.

Sappy time over. He'd had too much beer and he needed to get to bed and start on his own future. Who knew what it would bring, but he was ready for the challenge.

* * * *

"We should leave," Angel said reluctantly.

He really didn't want to leave the pleasure planet they'd been on for the last few weeks.

"Don't wanna," Frank groaned.

The trial was over, not that they really needed to do much. Frank had given his information over and that had been that. Chuck was on a prison planet as well as a few ex-Alliance members. Angel tried to feel sorry for them, but he really couldn't. They'd brought it on themselves.

"I promised Archer we'd help get him settled." He caressed Frank's sweaty back.

They were lying in the sun for some reason he didn't know. Frank had said it would be relaxing, but whatever. He'd rather be inside doing some naughty things to his lover. He wondered if he could lure him away from the beach.

"Oh, Archer is it now." Frank opened one eye and glared at him.

"What, you jealous?" Angel winked.

Frank snorted and closed his eyes.

"What, you could totally be jealous that he's after all of this." Angel rubbed a hand down his body.

Frank shot off his lounger and pulled Angel back to their room.

"This is why I have nothing to worry about."

Frank tugged his skimpy shorts down and threw them aside. He pushed Angel onto the bed and crawled up his body until Frank's hard dick was right in his face.

Now this was what Angel was talking about. He opened his mouth wide and waited for Frank to begin fucking his face. He hummed at the taste. Frank was like warm sunshine.

"You like that, don't you? I'm going to fuck you, Angel. Nobody else but me. Then later you're going to ride my ass so hard, I'll feel it all the way to the *Allora*. Jealous—oh, fuck—do that again."

Angel managed to laugh around Frank's cock until Frank thrust a bit too far and choked Angel. He gagged and Frank pulled out.

"Shit, damn it. I'm sorry."

He still laughed and pushed Frank down onto the bed, straddling his hips. "Now, what was it you were saying? You're going to fuck me—what if I want to make love to you first?"

"Angel—" Frank began to squirm underneath him.

"Yes, Frank?" Angel continued to touch any skin within reach. He rubbed his ass against Frank's dick but didn't attempt to touch it any other way.

"I want—" Frank was panting now.

"What do you want, Frank?"

Angel reached back and grasped Frank's cock, giving it a squeeze and running his thumb over the head.

"I need you, Angel."

"Need me to do what, Frank? Talk to me or I won't know."

Frank bucked in Angel's hands and almost unseated him. Angel gripped his thighs tighter around Frank's hips. He wasn't going anywhere.

"Let me in, Angel. Please."

"Since you asked so nicely." Angel leaned over to the side table where they'd left the lube that morning.

He put some on his fingers and played with his hole. Not that he needed it, but he loved how it felt. Frank joined in, his thumb right alongside Angel's finger. Frank hit his gland and he couldn't wait. He might want to, but he'd been craving this since they'd got to the beach earlier.

Angel pulled Frank's hand away and reached for his dick. He sat down on it, hissing as Frank's balls hit his ass.

"Move, Ang—fuck, move."

He rocked back and forth. Angel loved the noises that left Frank's mouth when they made love. It had him so hard he thought he'd burst without touching himself.

Frank didn't let him ride for long. Without losing contact he turned them both over until he had Angel's legs up on his shoulders. Angel grasped his hips and held on for the ride, meeting Frank thrust for thrust.

Then Frank slowed to a stop and just looked at Angel. He blinked up, almost shocked by the shift in mood. Frank took Angel's hands and interlaced their fingers, gripping them tight. He pulled out until only the tip rested inside Angel's hole then slid back in over and over—but slow, oh so fucking slow. He was killing Angel one stroke at a time, but he loved every second of it.

Frank licked Angel's lips before he kissed his forehead. Then Frank kissed his cheeks as well as his chin before nuzzling into Angel's neck. Every touch was given to Angel in love and he felt it in his very soul.

His orgasm was a slow-heated build, Frank thrust and thrust, riding through each shudder of Angel's body.

The only sound in the room was the light slap of bodies and their moans as they both came. Angel never even touched his cock. Just the friction from their bodies and the pumping of Frank's shaft had him coming harder than he ever had in his life.

Frank collapsed on Angel's chest and neither moved for a few minutes. Angel even fell asleep for a bit.

* * * *

When he opened his eyes, Frank was looking down on him.

"You know I love you, right?"

Angel propped himself up on the headboard. "Yes. I love you too."

"Okay. I just have to say it sometimes because it seems so unreal that I'm here with you. That I don't have to worry about doing anything illegal to get by. That I might be able to do something that will make my mom proud of me for a change. And, yeah, sometimes I need a pinch to know it's all really happening."

Angel pinched Frank's chest, twisting the nipple.

"Hey! Ouch."

"What? That wasn't a call for me to pinch you? Sounded like it to me." Angel chuckled.

"Smart ass."

"That's why you love me."

"No, that's why you think I love you."

"So, why do you love me?"

"Oh, let me count the ways?" Frank laughed. "Where should I start? You're loyal and would do anything for those you love. You install faith and trust in people who don't know you. You're sexy as fuck. Ahh—"

Angel rolled on top of Frank, sticking to his chest. They really should shower.

"You had me at sexy as fuck." Angel laughed against Frank's lips.

"And that there—how you can laugh and make things fun. I love that."

"You're loyal too, Frank."

"I was a criminal."

"Who was very loyal to his boss."

"Until I turned him in."

"He'd gone a bit off his rocker, Frank. You did what you thought was best in the situation."

"If I was truly loyal I would have—"

Angel covered Frank's mouth with another kiss to shut him up.

"This is my list and if I say you're loyal, you're loyal, damn it. Now, where was I, yes, loyal. You're also a hero."

"Am—"

Angel's glare cut Frank off and he pressed his lips shut.

"You have a big heart. Don't think I don't know about the orphanage that gets anonymous donations. Or the fact that you fully support your mom and sister so they can do whatever they want. How about that you followed your heart, but gave it to the wrong person leading you to a life you didn't belong in. Now all that has changed."

"Oh it has? I supposed you're the right person, the one my heart belongs to."

"Yep."

"Smug bastard."

"But I'm right, aren't I?" Angel nodded. "Now let's go shower. I'm all sticky." Angel pressed his mouth one more time to Frank's before hopping off the bed.

"Do we really have to leave?"

Frank didn't move off the bed. He had to be starting to itch. Angel knew he was. The shower was calling his name.

"We do. But just think, in a week it'll be just the two of us on the *Avenger*."

"Well, only until we pick up the crew."

"There is that, but we can go wherever we want."

"You like that, don't you? Exploring?"

"I do, that was the only thing I really enjoyed about my undercover gigs—going to different places, but now I don't have to sneak in. I can go all official."

"Whatever, you're totally going to put your ninja skills to use and you know it." Frank laughed.

"Okay, maybe. That part can be fun too, as long as someone's not trying to kill you."

"I like that part too. No more laser wounds. Or ships blowing up or…anything else."

"You shouldn't put that out there, because now it's totally going to happen." Angel snorted.

"Shut it." Frank shook his head and got off the bed.

"You know you love me, baby."

"I'll love you more if you shut it."

"You love my mouth too and all the wicked things it does to you."

"Maybe."

"I'll show you 'maybe'." Angel chased Frank into the bathroom.

* * * *

Frank had never been happier. He was afraid to jinx it. They'd left their tropical paradise and were docking on the *Allora*. This time he wasn't nervous and was happy to see Robert. The guy was so much like Angel it was almost scary.

It was just him, he knew that, but the ship looked different this time. Probably because he didn't have to be worried about being detained. Not that Angel would have let that happen. He told Frank he had a ship all ready for them to flee on if necessary.

He totally loved that man. They were there to greet Archer, but they were also there to get their first orders. Frank wasn't technically Alliance and never would be, not with his criminal record. Angel tried to get it all expunged, but Frank told him to leave it alone. He didn't need to be official to help.

They reached Robert's office and Angel knocked on the door.

"Enter."

"Hey, Dad. Where's your secretary?" Angel shut the door behind them.

"On a break. You ready to get going?" Robert stood and held out his hand for Frank before sitting on the edge of his desk.

"I think so. Where're you sending us?"

"Some outer rim planet that is having issues with pirates. I'd like to see what you can do to help. And you'll be needed back here soon for my retirement party and your brother's promotion."

"I'm sure we can manage."

Frank just sat back and watched the interaction. He could tell the men loved each other and it was nice to see. They finished their business and Robert walked with them to meet Archer. They'd beat him to the ship, but not by much.

"So what will Archer be training for?" Frank was curious.

The man seemed good with security issues, but Frank hadn't really got to know him very well. Not like Angel had.

"He's going to train under Alphonse. I'm hoping he can fill out Frost's post. We lost him when he tried to get Alphonse killed. He'd be helping with undercover ops, be their go-to guy."

"He should be good with that." Angel seemed pleased.

Frank really wasn't jealous—much. Archer was exotic—big and built to boot.

Archer entered the hall wiping his hands on his pants. He still had the air of sadness that clung to him when Frank had met him for the first time. Hopefully the *Allora* would be good to him.

Angel walked over and gave Archer a big hug. Frank followed.

"It's good to see a couple of familiar faces in this vast emptiness of space." Archer held out a hand for Robert.

"Good to see you, son. I have someone coming down to show you and the others to their quarters. They'll give you a tour of the ship, but your duties and studies won't start officially for a couple days so you can get acclimated to the ship. You'll be dropping me off at Alliance headquarters and my first mate will be in charge. I don't usually fly with the ship. I'll leave you guys to talk. I'll be seeing you soon, Tok."

Robert hugged Angel and Frank. "I'll talk to the both of you soon."

"Yes, sir." Angel nodded to Robert.

They'd already made plans to get together before Alphonse was sworn in.

"Frank and I will show you around before we leave." Angel waved off the ensign who'd shown up.

"How's Earth?" Angel kept the conversation going.

"It's good. Your brother and his partner are making plans to vacation there." Archer shook his head.

"Yeah, James is fascinated with the planet for some reason." Angel shrugged.

Frank didn't understand it either, but he guessed there was a lot of land left to explore. Voit's people hadn't populated the whole place, just a few spots. The Alliance was going to help by bringing in more technology and more people.

It would be fascinating to see where it would be in just a few short years, but purely from a distance. Frank had no desire to go back. He watched Angel's ass as they walked the corridors. He really wasn't paying attention when he ran into Archer's back.

He looked around to see what had stopped him only to find a slim, very pale blond man in a tight uniform walk by. Angel chuckled and kept walking. Frank just shook his head.

"No worries, man, there are plenty of pretty boys walking around the station." Angel patted Archer's back.

"Yeah—but, man, I'm so…different from everyone."

"What? How?" Frank was confused. All he saw was an attractive man in front of him. He might have given him a go if he wasn't with Angel.

"I'm purple." His tone suggested he wanted to follow that with a duh.

"And?" Angel shrugged. "I've seen all kinds of different species. You are *far* from different. You're sexy and exotic. Purple is the new white." Angel snorted.

"Be serious," Frank warned.

"I totally am. Listen, most people don't care. Everyone is unique in their own way."

"He's right, Archer." Frank was nodding.

"See, I can be serious." Angel ruined it by winking.

"I guess we'll see, won't we."

"You will. I think you being here will be good for you, Archer." Angel stopped at a door. "This is your cabin. Down the hall to the left is the mess hall. Back the way we came if you follow the hall, you'll run into the command centre. That's where you'll meet everyone in two days. Here is our personal com frequency. Call us. I mean it. If you need anything. Got it?"

"Got it. Thanks for this." Archer took the paper Angel had handed him and put it in his pocket.

"Okay, we're out of here, but my dad will take good care of you." Angel hugged him one last time.

"You'll be good. Like Angel said, call if you need us." Frank took his turn to hug the big guy.

"Thanks for everything." Archer nodded and went into the cabin, shutting the door behind him.

"He's really sad, huh? Homesick already?" Frank asked.

"More like Voit sick."

"Huh?"

"Yeah, he has a thing for Voit, but it wasn't returned. I think that's why he's here." Angel glanced back at the door.

Frank followed his gaze. Now he really hoped the man found what he was searching for.

"Ready for our new adventure?" Angel grinned.

"Lead the way and I'll follow." Frank smiled back.

About the Author

Jambrea wanted to be the youngest romance author published, but life impeded the dreams. She put her writing aside and went to college briefly, then enlisted in the Air Force. After serving in the military, she returned home to Indiana to start her family. A few years later, she discovered yahoo groups and book reviews. There was no turning back. She was bit by the writing bug.

She enjoys spending time with her son when not writing and loves to receive reader feedback. She's addicted to the internet so feel free to email her anytime.

Jambrea Jo Jones loves to hear from readers. You can find her contact information, website details and author profile page at http://www.total-e-bound.com.

Total-E-Bound Publishing

www.total-e-bound.com

Take a look at our exciting range of literagasmic™
erotic romance titles and discover pure quality
at Total-E-Bound.